Back in the Day

Back in the Day

OLIVER LOVRENSKI

Translated by Nichola Smalley

HAMISH HAMILTON
an imprint of
PENGUIN BOOKS

HAMISH HAMILTON

UK | USA | Canada | Ireland | Australia
India | New Zealand | South Africa

Hamish Hamilton is part of the Penguin Random House group of companies
whose addresses can be found at global.penguinrandomhouse.com

Penguin Random House UK,
One Embassy Gardens, 8 Viaduct Gardens, London SW11 7BW

penguin.co.uk

First published in Norwegian as *Da vi var yngre* by Aschehoug 2023
This edition published by Hamish Hamilton 2025

001

Copyright © Oliver Lovrenski, 2023
Translation copyright © Nichola Smalley, 2025

The moral right of the copyright holders has been asserted

Published by agreement with Salomonsson Agency

Image #6991139 created by Uswa KDT from Noun Project

Lyrics from 'Lullaby Freestyle' by Lars Reiersen. Lyrics from 'Graveyard Shifts'
by Tyr Markus Røe. Lyrics from 'Happy' by Pharrell Williams.

This translation has been published with the financial support of NORLA

No part of this book may be used or reproduced in any manner for the
purpose of training artificial intelligence technologies or systems. In accordance
with Article 4(3) of the DSM Directive 2019/790, Penguin Random House
expressly reserves this work from the text and data mining exception

Set in 11.5/15.6pt Calluna
Typeset by Jouve (UK), Milton Keynes
Printed and bound in Great Britain by Clays Ltd, Elcograf S.p.A.

The authorised representative in the EEA is Penguin Random House Ireland,
Morrison Chambers, 32 Nassau Street, Dublin D02 YH68

A CIP catalogue record for this book is available from the British Library

ISBN: 978–0–241–70583–4

Penguin Random House is committed to a sustainable future
for our business, our readers and our planet. This book is made from
Forest Stewardship Council® certified paper.

for all the nights
i dont remember enough of
with the people i can never forget

TO ALL OF YOU

who shared warm fanta
and cold kebab
tins of snus and packs of tabs

and cheap jokes
when that was all we had

and TO EVERYONE

too busy keeping
their story alive
to tell it

may we one day
forgive ourselves

for everything
said, done and forgotten

brother
last night i got woke up by marco ringing, and he was crying, he said, he died ivor, he died, and i didnt need to hear who to know, i just hung up

BRUDDAS

fryctur and evry-day racism.

nooku! i clocked why people gonna watch the 6clock stuff. it all started when we got pirated soundtrack to go get sonic munch. but like, whaty soundtrak, is no problem cuz we just eat kebab abour pizza. but now wrestaling paper the opponant. has got to say yo, know more moovy more pronouns.

so basically thatt batle question whati wroo'd say because the worlds biggest held asoud withour fini-stry best. cos first arran said he wanta siking, but onlooy just wani. nah. battis vo moos. and then I shoold say 'yeah', said 'ho, s forget it. today we bo' mughti'. and then the wa'ofworld. breake out in th' lndulgi of pressures. and were abour to start a new argu-salting, when, what ditis out. it dus the tiny little high voice of Sanit nam trangelth i wantt to have i-F-female. and sayss fine. what, cali-men female. and he crosses his arms and waits. to'afterris the mutational dish. dont be racist.

fenelår and everyday racism
today i clocked why people go to war over the dumbest stuff, it all started when we got hungry, so aight, lets go get some munch, but like, what? normally its no problem cos we just eat kebab, share pizza, but now were making paper the opportunities opened up you know, more money more problems

so basically that little question what we gonna eat became the worlds biggest beef about whose country is best, cos first arjan said he wants indian, but marco just went, nah, bariis iyo moos, and then i shook my head, said, boys forget it, today we go croatian, and then the war of words breaks out in the middle of gunerius, and were about to start a new arab spring, when jonas calls out in this tiny little high voice, what about me yeah, i want to have f-f-fenalår, and were like, what you mean fenalår, and he crosses his arms and says, fenalår, its the n-national dish, dont be racist

the ladder 1
and in year ten before i became a proper fiend and still
had normal friends we got some xannies, and if you
know you know, when you take one, you take another,
and then you might as well take them all, and in the end
i was on my way through the second tray and fell asleep
on the sofa and didnt wake up, and i was meant to be
meeting a friend, and he knew i was messing with them
things, so when i didnt answer he got a ladder to the
window and was banging and saw me lying on the sofa
all pale while he was on the phone to marco and was
about to call 113

luckily he managed to open one of the windows and
climbed in, then shook the life back in me

when i woke up, he was standing over me with
tears on his cheeks, he said, ivor, i love you,
but i cant take no more

candyflip
marco called in the middle of class like, bro did you hear arjan baxed two wasteman in the classroom, wallah the cops got him, so i asked what happened, and apparently arjan had woke up thought the suns grinning the earths spinning time for a candyflip, cos after first period he was in the pisser for forty minutes, and when he came back, he had no top on and was shouting about everyone being friends and love on earth, then two pakis started shouting fucking homo, and arjan was like, yeah, what if i am, and threw a table at one and dropped the other with a knuckleduster, and then the feds came, and i was facetiming arjan as he sat in the back of the wagon with white walls, airing out his nipples, face one big smirk, i asked, wagwan, but he just shook his head and said, bro, you ever think about how all lives are worth the same, tomorrow ima go vegan

happy families 1
we was in beirut on a lowkey diss battle, and first marco was like, hey jonas you look such a child all you can bang is paedos, and its actually kinda true cos a few times old men came up to him and started chatting, but you know jonas wasnt giving up so he was like, yeah, and your foreheads b-b-blacker and b-bigger than my tv when its t-turned off, and then all the boys shouted ohhhh burn, cos jonas has actually got the biggest tv of anyone, its a 65 inch samsung with built in netflix, so then marco took off his jacket and got fucking serious, but before he could say shit, arjan steps in and goes, yeah, but at least his forehead dont get slapped by his dad, and even then we said oooh burn, but a bit lower cos it was actually kinda harsh, and all the boys looked at jonas like, you gonna let him chat to you like that, so jonas gets up, like, yeah but at least my d-d-dad wanted to have me, and then even ali behind the counter shouted burn, cos everyone knows arjan lives in a home and maybe his dad didnt want him

. . . this shit is mad, for my guys ive been a brudda, friend and fucking dad
in preschool dad was a goldsmith, soldier, astronaut and pirate, or really he just wasnt there, but pirate was cooler

la familia
arjan and jonas, i dont know them so well yeah, not like marco, but like, to be honest, its a month since marco went college and they started chilling with us, not so weird man dont know their favourite food and that, get me, and anyway, when you a crew like that you get to know each other bare fast, especially with the drugs things go quick, one trip and it feels like you known each other for like five years yeah, and we musta done eleven already, so whats that? at least fifty

the problem
sometimes marco annoys me you know, today he called and woke me up so early it was unreal, he goes, i just seen your story, how much you take yesterday? i told him i took the rest of the e, and he was like, how much, four and a half, he said, ivor, you ever think you might have a problem? i said to him, fucks wrong with you man, people with stones shouldnt throw marbles, youre no better, and he goes, yeah i am, ivor, and the fact you cant see it, thats the problem

ola starr
first time i met jonas was on a stairwell behind the sweet shop at bislett stadium across the street from lille-b

it was right at the start of sixth form, id been there maybe four or five days, and me and marco was sitting on the steps grinding chronic while we waited for a kid he knew from college

i remember i said, is that him, my voice kinda shocked, cos this boy was so little and pale with white hair, and real nervous like he was about to speak in front of the class, but marco went yeah, and walaalkay – give him a chance, cos even if hes a little different, when you get to know him, wallahi billahi, you gonna feel him

i said aight, cos i trust marco, and if you look at us now, you see marco was right

polo

and actually marcos name aint marco, its liban, liban mohammed ali, which i actually think is kinda messed up, cos if hed been a boxer hed have had almost the same name as the goat, but like everyone just calls marco marco, and i aint gonna lie i think a lot of people dont even know his real name, like jonas and arjan know now for sure, cos we told them the whole story, but for a long time they didnt know shit

what happened was that i was in the first class of little school, and one day marco came to norway and started school in the same class as me, and cos at the start he didnt really speak much norwegian, he was kind of an outsider that not many people chatted to, and cos of that he was trying to get people to laugh, but getting laughs aint too easy when you dont chat the same language, so one day when we was sitting in class he stood up and shouted marco! like from that vine of two people standing in the sunflowers, and one shouts marco, and the other one jumps in the air and shouts polo, so out in real life when someone shouts marco, someone else gotta be like polo, and i knew everyone had seen the video cos when it first came out everyone would call out, but now no one was making a sound, so in the end i got up and was like POLO! so loud it made the teacher jump for real, and even if we was on the way to the headteacher, the brother smiled so wide the hallways didnt need no lamp, and after that when i saw him in gym class, i was like marco! and he called back polo! and from then on instead of saying hi, every morning i called out marco! and he answered polo! and thats how we got to be brothers, and how he got his name

el chapo
we was gonna be 2pac and zlatan and jordan and tyson and elden and banksy and founders like musk so it wasnt dreams we was lacking but hope and so here we are turning into chapo

jonas lil bro 1
jonas dad was off boozing again, so we was at his
yard, drinking, and after a bit marco was like, jonas,
why dont you live at your mums instead, with your
lil bro, and jonas got serious and said, we used to
unt-t-til i was like fourteen, but then he m-m-moved
out and mum couldnt handle having both of us, so i
came with him, and one time my nose g-got broke,
and i said i got smacked by a football in pe, but when
i was with mum at maccie ds i was crying i said, mum
i want to come home, and she actually said fine you
can come, and i was so happy like the world glowed
a thousand c-colours at once, and i said ill always
tidy my room and take the rubbish out, even without
you asking, and then mum said, youre a good boy,
tomorrow well get your things, and it was better than
ecstasy i swear, the whole of maccie ds was like a
d-disco

jonas lil bro 2
arjan was like, so fam, you was gonna move home, escape that shit, what happened? jonas took a sip, he said, m-mum came with the car, i ran out with my backpack and then in again to get my pokemon cards, but when i came out, l-lil bro was going in yeah, he was like, hi, i said, m-mum w-whats he doing here, she said, come on jonas, you know i cant have both of you, so i said, nah its cool, id rather live with d-dad

ive seen babies being born and ive seen my friends die
after that we all had a silent agreement, enough family
chat and instead we talked about music and jonas
went, hey you know who larsiveli is? i started listening
to him, and we was like, yeah, everyone knows who
veli is bro, are you dumb, your dad knows who veli is,
but he just went, n-no, i shown h-h-him yesterday and
he didnt know, and then marco facepalmed and sent
a secret #pray4jonas in the chat, but he put lullaby
freestyle on and all the man got emotional

i ♡ school 1
not gonna lie school is such a messed up business, like sixth form just started and mans already done you know, and every morning i wake up and think maybe it was all just some fucked up bad dream and im actually twenty years old in croatia with five baddies, baby oil and three pepperoni pizzas, but nah, i still have to go school and learn why some stones are different colours

shottas
we had nothing to do so we linked by the station, and marco teefed some booze so we all had a few sips except jonas cos marco refused to pass him the bottle, and jonas said it wasnt fair he didnt get none, but marco said nah, shots are for shottas

hopeless to be hopeless
we bumped into the headteacher from our old school,
and he remembered us, no surprises there, so we said
hello and were actually bout to bounce when he asked
me, you were going to be a lawyer, hows it looking,
and i didnt know what to say, but marco saved me,
he said, its hopeless, and were not giving up

the net under the sun over the water
between the national museum and aker brygge, on the waterfront in front of the city hall, theres this little corner of the oslo fjord called pipervika, and theres this pier there, or theres bare piers, but its this one thats special, cos theyve cut big holes in it, and in the holes they put nets, like for fishing, except these are for people, and the water laps underneath, and the sun shines above, so almost every time were tripping on acid or e, we take a little tour down to the net and float over the sea

i ♡ school 2
and it dont help that me and marco dont go same school no more, after we did all the way since we was tiny, every single day sitting in the same classroom, getting smart, creating chaos, and now hes some place learning to build houses, while im sitting here in german 2 and social studies cos that way youre keeping your options open

ea7 and jordans

not gonna lie i cant remember a life without marco, sometimes in little school the other kids said, hey how come youre brothers, you dont even look like each other, and marco freaked a bit, like hey, what you mean we dont look like each other, and we played dumb like we didnt know, even though we knew the whole time it was cos marco looks like abdi from under the bridge and i look like vladimir who can paint your house but only cash my friend, only cash

and even though were both tall, hes thinner with this massive afro that never gets wet on the inside, and a few times hes hid baggies in it, but he mostly just has an afro comb, and i aint got a fro, ive got the shortest balkan fade like i was one of the boys off the croatian national team except i cant play football cos in year five i strained my groin and i aint got no pace and that, and marcos normally in his ea7 jacket with the zip open and his kenzo sweater under it which is blue and the only thick jumper he has, cos he spends all his floos on hash, kebabs and snus, and then hes always got those blue jordans, cos theyre the only shoes he has, and when they got a hole in, we taped them up with black tape we taxed from kjell & company, cos then it wouldnt show so much, or, it shows a bit but whatever, who the fucks looking under his shoes anyway

cafe politicians
when we was in little school, marco took me to a cafe
in grønland a few times after school cos his uncle was
always there, and if it was summer and the sun was
out abti-marco was a real g and would give us twenty
kroner for ice cream, and wed bounce to the shop and
get a joystick cola, eight kroner, and if he was in an
extra next level good mood, hed give us twenty each (!)
and wed grab the worlds best ice cream, come back, our
faces all smiles

but for the money abti would always deal out life
lessons, like do well in school you can be politician,
make good impact, and if you want a good xaas, you
must a few times swallow the pride and thats fine

the first time marco took me there we was seven, eight,
and i got a little nervous, not gonna lie, cos in the
cafe there was all them older guys round every table,
waving their arms and talking so loud they was almost
shouting, and i understood zero cos it was all somali,
but it mostly looked like they was about to go to war, so
i asked marco, whats going on, he said, chill bro, its just
fadhi ku dirir

addictive personalities
they say some people have addictive personalities, and i think arjan fits, cos after he started bunning, we was sitting in dominos and sharing a bit of pizza with water, counting floos to get some hash, and when we found out we didnt have enough, he started crying

paracet
first time marco drank a lot we was about thirteen and got proper wasted, the next day i called like, whats up, he said, im never drinking again wallahi, my heads got the achies

shotta soul
arjan was like, you stress so much about money, just smoke a jay and chill innit, marco said, fuck that hippy shit, i grew up with toast for dinner and pyjamas on ski days wallah, ima die before i go broke again

all animals have equal value but
when i was little i wanted to be a lawyer, have my own company with my name on a big sign over the door so everyone knew who was boss, and marco would have an office next door, and in reception wed have the pengest shorty in a grey skirt, and when we went into court, everyone would be going like, owww its them man, judge gonna get fucked!

cos since little school me and marco been top of the class, maths, norwegian, english, ict, everything, we ran shit, got ahead, and in class we put our hands up, after school we studied, shit we even read at night, rung each other up like, what did you get for that question, what about that one, and we tested each other on fractions

but after a while we started getting bored, like come to class already read the whole textbook, so we went to the teachers and said give us harder work to do, but they was like no, its better if everyone does the same cos we dont want to create differences, and marco said god created differences so everyone would be different, and i said fucking communist cos i heard it at the polling station, but still they didnt want to listen, so in every class we already knew everything and had nothing to do, but we had to do something, so we talked, created a little chaos, and then the teachers freaked, and dont get me wrong, im not saying that was all of it, but a hundred per cent its part of the reason we got more steam to let off than asian aunties at the laundrette

8
in year ten we was by the metro with some next man
after school, just blazing, then we said safe yeah, see you
in the morning, but in the morning he wasnt there, so i
called like bro, you sick again or what haha, but he was
like nah, got sent away man, when you back, 3 years,
what, you fucking with me, no, for real

the week after this other guy got sent to a home too,
both brothers since way back, like day one, and now it
was year ten and poof, they was gone

before i could count on one hand who got sent,
now i need an octopus man

oh, you want some 1
we was on the metro telling stories and marco told us about
the first time he and arjan met, it was his second day at
college and they was going on some trip or whatever, so the
whole class were sitting on the tram when arjan ran over to
marco who was sitting there munching his baguette, and
theyd never spoken before but arjan grabbed it off him, ran
to the front of the carriage and started eating, and of course
marco ran after, about to get the first detention of the year,
he shouted, fucks wrong with you, and arjan looked up
with his mouth full of food, said, oh, you want some

oh, you want some 2
and youre probably thinking arjan did that cos hes a
dumbass or something, but swear down, he just dont
get it, no one does, childrens services have been trying
for twelve years this summer and still they dont get shit,
and after the story marco said to arjan, wallahi you need
to start behaving yourself, if santa exists youre going on
the list of naughty kids, and arjans like, ok good, if santa
exists youve got a permanent place on the blacklist

when we left maccie ds two hours later, jonas woke up
from his high and said what you mean, blacklist, and
arjan was like yeah, cos hes black

oh, you want some 3
after arjans blacklist joke marco pranked him as
payback he dashed some molly in his fanta before his
first presentation in class

be quiet be quiet 1

when everyone talks different languages, its natural we learn from each other, like i learned a bit of somali and arabic from marco and his family from early, but after jonas and arjan came into the picture, we also had to teach them a few basic things in croatian and arabic, like be quiet, run, feds are coming, grab this or that etc, and even if it took bare time, they learned in the end, and its well smart if for example the wrong persons standing next to you so you cant talk

and today was a situation like that, cos me and marco were sitting in the opera house with this colombian gyal hes seeing when arjan and jonas rocked up, and arjan who was high on illicit substances thought that in front of him was a girl hed linked the previous weekend, but brother was arjan wrong

so while arjan was thanking mariah for a great time and asking if theyd enjoyed the restaurant, marco started shout-whispering, *skot skot*, and arjan, whod forgotten what that meant, thought he was saying she didnt speak norwegian and did this mad apology (in norwegian), turned back to the girl, pointing first at himself, then at her, and said in English: ME arjan, YOU mariah, HOW – ARE – YOU?

be quiet be quiet 2
mariah (gabriella) got up and shouted, what the fuck is wrong with you, and ran her mascara ran too

marco asked how hard it was to remember a simple word, arjan replied that we was in norway now, and if marco wanted to make himself understood, he should speak norwegian

pola-pola
last time i was in the old country, i was at this corner shop, and the guy who worked there was like jesi li ti odavde (are you from here), and so i said, pola-pola, hrvatski i norveški, imam obitelj odavde (i have family from here), so then he asked if i was visiting them, my family, but i was just like, theyre . . . whats the word (cos i didnt know it), and he said holiday? and i went nah, dead

first time for everything 1
marco went, meet at majorstuen school? i texted back fine, he said bring arjan, we got there and jonas and marco were on the swing smoking a joint, jonas with a bleeding nose and soon-to-be-black eye and marco with a torn shirt and fucked up afro, i shouted, wagwan, you lot get jumped, but they shook their heads and jonas went, w-w-we had a 1-on-1 with each other, i said what, whats wrong with you why, marco laughed and said, fighting is like getting fucked, the first time should be with someone you trust

brothers
they say brothers? you lot aint brothers, man you aint even family, but if were not family, why is it us we call every time we cant ring no one else, why is it us whos there when no one else is, fuck you not family, if were not family, tell me why were the only ones we can chat to about the things no one else saw, no one else heard, you know – all the things family should never do

gdje si, srce moje?
when i was little, the whole fam was always
celebrating things like birthdays and christmas,
and when we made a circle round the tree, holding
hands and singing, the circle was even big enough
to go round the whole thing, swear down, full
disney christmas with pork belly, old style meatballs,
christmas sausage, best thing ive tasted, and
then destroy the homemade krumkake cookies,
woahwoahwoah that slapped bro!

and when it was summer and Baba and me were back
in the old country, suddenly five cousins all rocked up
from norway, all together in the house with a garden
and barbecue and card games and no-i-dont-want-no-
suncream, and at night we watched boxing matches
with one earpiece each, like dont move too much cos
youll pull mine out, mobile up over your head right by
the window, cos this is the balkans bro, you want signal,
get on the roof

every summer we was there for two months,
me and Baba, just on our twos almost the whole
time, shed give me pocket money, and while she was
working on the computer id cycle round on the little

streets and beaches buying fries and energy drinks,
sitting on the wall round the village in the sun staring
at the blue sky and the white boats and sharing food
with the cats, and some things you dont tell no one,
but i miss her

sixty-eights 1
when i was little and wanted to be a boxer, i got my
first gloves and pads, and i was at Babas a few days
a week, and at times she lived with us, and even if
she was a pacifist and a hippy and help the children
and the usas the devil, she still taught herself how
to hold the pads so she could train with me, and we
stood in the living room with her saying one, one-
two, double jab, crossbody, and when i got new gloves
we even sparred, swear down, she put on gloves like
it was rocky 6

even if she hated violence and fighting, and i mean,
really hated it, she still trained with me for hours,
laughing, smiling, warm laughter bouncing off the
walls, i was six, then seven, eight, she said, just you
wait, youre gonna knock them out cold, my boy, so
when she got sick it was rough as, cos she was always
the strong one

1st day at work 1
jonas is my brother, but not gonna lie, hes in the wrong scene

today man was in town, me, jonas, marco (arjans on house arrest), when suddenly two dots on opposite sides of town were in urgent need, and after a few ifs and buts it ended up with jonas going to meet one of the guys

so while me and marco reached this one man, jonas boosted to the other, and the whole time my heart was in my throat thoughts whirling cos jonas never even delivered a pizza and theres a reason for that, but like usual marco was doing some family therapy, he goes, trust him man wallah he aint a kid no more, and im thinking aight, hows he gonna fuck this up still, and then the phone rings and in this shaky little voice jonas goes, yeah, something h-happened, the shits g-g-gone

1st day at work 2
it would be one thing if jonas got jacked by twelve older man with machetes and planes and tanks and he was fighting tooth and nail to the last breath like some legendary fighter, but no, my man just said i forgot my ps, just gonna go get em, and jonas said, oh yeah sounds great, ill just wait here, and surprise surprise, guy never came back

so after that we had to spend half the day finding this little snake, ringing round, checking out a couple of stoner spots in town, but no, still nothing

in the end marco saw a story one of my mans crew put up with pictures of them blazing, and all the guys freaked out like, awww theyre posting our shit still, are they dumb or what, dont they know, they forgot who we was, and marco was like, yeah wallah, today families gonna weep and people gonna get buried, and so we bounced straight there and went off at them, but we didnt really go off that much, just like, kiss my shoes, hand over the cash plus two hundred, and filmed it after, cos like bro – we pulled this one a hundred times ourselves, we cant be hypocrites now can we

1st day at work 3

not gonna lie, it was jonas who caught most chaos, marco going off on him all day, you know marco was the one who first took him in, and so hes his responsibility a bit, you know, hes the one who adopted, hes the one whos gotta go off

marco even turned on his good norwegian, and he only does that when hes serious, but also its fucking jokes cos suddenly he sounds like this old norwegian teacher with glasses round his neck and a grey beard, swear down, you shoulda heard him, like: jonas, im so disappointed by your behaviour, youre a complete and utter dimwit, completely without normal competencies, basic knowledge, critical thinking etc etc

entrepreneurial spirit
we started blazing in year nine, and after we got a
plug and grabbed from him for a few months he said,
you kids know a lot of man who bunn, right, and we
said, yeah of course, and he goes aight, you lot wanna
make a little paper? afterwards me and marco copped
our first zed of hash, my man showed us a gram, point
eight is better, cos then you earn a little more, after
that he handed us the bar, said great, do your thing, but
remember, if you lot lose it, youre done, we went, yeah
yeah, hundred per cent, imagine, we was proper shook,
but anyway, we had it in this snus tin, got rid of it, came
back, got a new pack, boom we got our first taste of
floos, and yalla, look at us now

map and compass
and a few months later we was in school when someone
went yo, heard the feds gonna be coming in with dogs,
and you know marco and i checked each other like
two man on the run, like owww, we gonna get caught,
pen for life, so we ran to the forest behind school and
started digging, must have been half a metre of mud
before we dropped the bar and the shank and the scales
and the bags of floos, snus, gerros, skins, after that we
filled it with earth and sprint back, and when we got to

school, we saw man was right cos the whole place was packed with feds and dogs and probably a helicopter too, but anyway that one teacher asked, what were you doing in the forest, and marco was like, its gym today, we had orienteering

animals travel the world
and one time marcos old lady found a pack and some ps in his room, and a few hours later we was sitting in beirut and marco just flipped like, those daddys boys be dropping out and going faajofaajo while were sitting here with used snus and zero floos, is it weird were fucking trapping huh

6 loaves 2 eggs and 400ml love
we was in croatia in her house, in the living room with the windows and doors all wide open, and it was before it happened, i was little, maybe ten, sitting at the dining table while she was in the kitchen with nuff plates and frying pans and fresh white bread from the bakers making french toast, and ive tasted french toast before and ive tasted french toast since, but ive never tasted french toast like i had that day, i must have eaten twenty slices, maybe more, i can still feel them in my stomach when its windy and im running for the bus, and she asked, you want more, i answered, yeah, and it went on like that without end, cos for some reason it never ran out and i never got sick of it, and it was real good times that stuck in my head and my heart and i still dont know what she put in the mix, if it was sugar, cardamom, ecstasy or just love

Baba
it was last year and i was in school when mum called, she said, you have to come to the hospital, it could happen any moment, and i went, what, now? the doctor said she had two years left still, that was like a week ago, what kind of calendar are these people using, who taught them maths?

but fine, i bounced, she couldnt speak, they said her whole body is really hurting now, everything hurts, so in a sense shes not here, i said nothing, the whole family there like when we was little at christmas, mum said, if you want to say something to her you should do it now, i whispered, youre the worlds best Baba, she was like, mmm

later that evening id been walking around the hospital for hours, copping little packs of pancakes from the different wards, and then i went to her room, the family around Babas bed, hugging and crying. it was dark, i thought i like it when they hug and dont fight, it would be better if they did it more often

the funeral
i was one of the coffin bearers, so heavy, when we
walked down between the pews in the church, everyone
checking us, i thought, i cant cry now, gotta be strong
for mum

and a few weeks back the old lady said, it started the
next day, the day after Baba died, that was when you
changed

feet without socks
jonas took gina for the first time, and right after we copped some vodka in helsfyr and had a chugging competition, then all of a sudden jonas was lying on the ground not breathing so good, and he was getting colder and colder like feet without socks, so i called 113 while marco dumped the rest and arjan was crying cos the chugging competition wasnt so important anymore and jonas had blue lips, and now hes in the hospital and says its all good only his dad went off on him

nydalen t (banen)
some things you dont tell no one, like how sometimes
when youre at the station and you hear the rush
in the tunnel, you take a step back, tense your body
and hold your breath, and when the trains passed and
youre still standing there, you wonder if youre ever
gonna dare to fly

sixty-eights 2
i was eleven, and we drove in the little green car to get
food, just us two, you could only drive the way wed
come, it was one way get me, but then this massive
truck rolled up, must have had forty wheels, and like
boom, blocked the whole road and wanted to get
through, but Baba didnt have anywhere to turn around,
and anyway it was this loser whod driven wrong,
but suddenly my man jumped out of the truck, huge
fucking guy, truck driver and all that, and he started
going off, and some people might have got shook but
Baba she just got out, started yelling back, real balkan
lady, you get me, she was almost seventy too, in one
of them house dresses with a knitted sweater over,
wooden clogs and glasses round her neck, standing with
her finger pointing in his face, like, ive got my grandson
in the car, youre not coming over here screaming at us!
and in the end, the guy boosts back to the truck, starts
reversing, Baba comes back, she goes: i cant stand that
kind of thing, i simply cant

beer iyo injera
i remember when we was little, sometimes marco
would rock up to school with hungry eyes and the
biggest grin, hed say, old lady done it yesterday, she
baked and now its rising!

four days later the alarm went off at 5:45, and after
the worlds quickest shower and on with the clothes,
i sprinted through the forest to marcos block, he said,
its risen, its risen and now shes frying it, the kitchen
all orange from the sun, marcos old lady was standing
at the stove and all his sisters round the table, with his
old man at one end, i washed my hands, found my spot
next to marco and tucked a white ikea napkin into my
jumper real careful

hi ivor, did you sleep well, she asked
yes habo, thanks habo
mmmmmm
she served up two great mounds of food, then water,
and black qaxwa for the old man

bismillah, and one after the other we each
helped ourselves to a fresh injera, the parents
and marcos big sisters with beerka la shiilay

and shaah, and the two of us with nesquik
and pale syrup bought on offer in sweden, cos
chicken-liver-what-no-hooyoo-i-dont-want-any

the siblings put on a show, marcos father asked me how
things were at home, all good wiilkey?

yes abti, all good

timetable

we meet up like every day, either right after school or if were not feeling school, we just meet when we get up like two or three in the afternoon, and together we eat a big breakfast like kebab pizza burger or fried chicken, and after that we either do what needs doing or just spend the day rushing and rolling, mostly ghb booze or speed, and then a couple of times a week e or crystal or acid ket mushies 2cb snow or something else fun, but we try not to drink too much cos then its just havoc still, and plus its not good for your liver

the fuck you up to
you know sometimes we chill at jonas place yeah, so today we was there chilling, and after a bit his lil bro was there too, but in the living room and we was in the bedroom, no need to bother the guy either, we know when youre gaming you just wanna game innit, but anyway we was sitting in jonas room, and he was in the living room talking to his lil bro, cos we was about to bounce and he was going to their grandmas cos their pops was on the way home, and jonas never lets his pops and his little brother meet, so while they was chatting marco was rolling a jay as per, and you know in jonas pops flat theres been chaos in the past, dope girls overdoses flaming bows and arrows over the blocks, you name it we done it, and jonas was along for the ride, but today he came into the room and said, lets bounce, but when he saw marco billing the jay, he fucking snapped and shouted, the fuck you up to, dont bring that shit here, my lil bros here

mum
no question it wasnt easy for mum and all, already way too much work, like when i was little in nursery, the last one getting picked up, standing with the staff, peering over the fence, they said, im sure shell be here soon, then, time passing, overtime, long time, dinner time, night time, but she always came, every time without exception, and its fine, cos she wanted to give me a better hand than she got dealt

but then Baba got sick, then Baba died, i got into chaos, the rest of the family was gone, and who was there for us, no one, nix

but i can do it bro, you know that
its just mum, shes the strongest person ive ever met, i swear, but maybe she got a little too much more than she should have

studying law 1
when i started sixth form, i said fine, mans gonna
take it serious, or at least go to all the classes, do my
projects, a little homework and that, and i was for real,
swear down, at the start man even ran around with this
fucking backpack, like who does that, marco was just
like bro, you turned into dora the explorer wagwan? but
i got good grades, in the little tests we had at the start
of the term, in law i got a 6, yeah, i even put my hand up
like, boom boom boom, the teacher said, such a great
insight, ivor! she saw me, you get me, just like, if you
continue this way youll get a lot out of this year, youll
probably end up with a solid 6, i said to her, i used to
want to be a lawyer, she said, you still can if you want to

clean counter
and when i decided to be a nerd, i said i was gonna
get clean too, so i downloaded clean counter, which
is this app that counts the days weeks months years
since you stopped getting high, and then it sends
motivational notifications or wow youve been clean
for 1 week today woohoo treat yourself to a cake, and
sometimes i still get those notifications cos i never
told them i failed again

off the wagon
being clean was going great until arjan and jonas were
gonna cop some hash, and i went with them cos hash
and green is no sweat, i just have a gerro instead, but
the problem was the plug was out of kif, but she had
amy, so then they went to cop that instead, and i went
along anyway, up to the flat, felt the itching in my gut
when i saw the powder, a rushing in my ears, they
bought point five, we went down to the courtyard and
sat on a bench, i said to them im not having any

they cut up the lines, my hands were sweating and my
head was roaring so loud i couldnt think, just sat with
my eyes on a bush to one side and tried to count the
leaves, i heard them sniff up the stripes and sigh, that
sigh like when youve had to piss for five hours, but held
on cos the bathrooms are rank, but now youre home
and can finally breathe out

inside me was the biggest battle between the side of
me that wanted to do good things, and the other side
saying,
chill man no stress, take one last bump
and you can quit tomorrow

*

arjan said, you want some, i was like, aight,
but just a half

when i get buzzed after a long time, its like i get tunnel
vision like a horse on a racetrack, and the only thing
that exists is how to forget as much as possible as quick
as possible

when we was done snorting, we went upstairs again
and bought everything she had which was eleven or
twelve grams, and in the end my nose was bleeding like
crazy, apple watch saying i hadnt slept for 67 hours and
in outpatients they said arjan was having a psychotic
episode

wa inaan xaaro
and in middle school we had spanish, and every time
you were thirsty or needed to take a dump, the teacher
forced you to ask in spanish, for example if i wanted
to bunn a zoot i had to use the excuse puedo llenar el
inodoro? (may i use the lavatory)

and after a bit it was getting annoying, at least for
people who couldnt speak spanish, so one day when
marco needed a dump, the whole thing ended with him
throwing a book at the teacher and shouting, next time
you gotta use the bathroom, come tell me i need to shit
in somali you cunt

white niggaz

some next man from frogner came to cop off us, and you know marco says nigga a lot, like yo nigga later nigga chill nigga whats good nigga, and he says it to everyone, white black whatever, so when these dudes show up, three or four proper west side types, polo shirts, zero pigment, he says it to them too, then later when we bounce, one of them shouts after us, yeah! later then nigga

marco turned around, hes like, dafuck you say to me, this guy said, relax man, when in rome, and then marco chased him into a courtyard and i heard shouts and punches like, fuck rome, youre in oslo nigga

you or me
i was young when i started carrying a blade, fourteen,
maybe thirteen, not gonna lie, to begin with no one
needed it either, we was mostly just playing hard, yeah
even if there was beef, and a couple of times it saved the
day, but mostly it just felt fire, safe you get me, like next
time someone tries to jack you, youre not getting jacked

and in the beginning there was this thrill and all,
your boys like owww, let me hold it yeah, afterwards
everyone posting pictures in private stories with a
machete like they was in the jungle, and maybe patting
you on the shoulder like, mans bad yo, mans rambo

but thats way back, now mans always got it, and i read
the news, the comments and that, people dont get it, i
know that, they think its a bad thing to carry a shank,
and maybe it is, but its not good getting wet either is it,
its you or me g, and i swear, youre not winning this one

bando baby
and the first time man pulled a shank on someone – so
shook, head nearly bursting from the adrenaline, legs
shaking, but then i felt like a badman, people all like
yooo, was it you who smacked up that one man, is it
true, he started crying la la la

after i thought wow somethings gonna change, like id
grown a bit or something, but no, i mean, it wasnt like
man suddenly was a robber, a criminal or whatever, i
was just me, get me, we didnt think like them people
in the news, gms and that, so dramatic, a little weed,
airpods, a puffa, creps, its not even really a robbery, like
the nokas heist, thats a robbery, we watched the film in
class, them man was on a mad ting

and thats how the world works, you a wasteman, you
lose, so in the end you either turn it around, say aight
no need to come find me, ill find you, get eaten, or be
the eater
done, khalas

silah

yesterday we took the green bus out of town to meet
a guy and sort out a silah, you know, bang bang, i
had marco and arjan with me, everything went well,
afterwards we split back to the city, snuck into a gym,
checked it out properly, the boys in turn, you talkin to
me, why you playing nice, man felt fly, like blood was
boiling, everyone with big smirks, a girl we knew was
working there, otherwise it was empty, we went out,
pointed it at her, lining up, she was like, not here! then
she held it, asked, you got enemies, i said, your man if
he finds out about us

we went and tested it out in the forest a few days later,
it was heavy, didnt know how loud the bang was before
the bang went off, and when it went off, man didnt hear
shit for days, the teacher asked questions, pointed at the
board, it said inheritance law, i heard beeeeep

ich verstehe nicht was du meinst
today in second period the community counsellor came and took me out of class cos apparently there was an attempted murder last night and the guy got shot in the shoulder, so now the feds was here with twenty-one questions like 50 cent, but i said the same to them as i said to the german teacher when i fucked up my exam, and in the end they let me go

jonas grandma 1
so jonas has a grandma he often goes to when his pops is on one, and since grandmas getting a bit old, she just moved into this apartment for old folks, so we was there unpacking boxes, and when we was done, we got frikadellen and waffles for dessert, and while we was munching away and trying not to make a mess, marco asked how the new place was, and jonas grandma said, well its lovely, its just that these teenagers hang around outside, and marco asked, oh right, what about them and she said, well, they call out nasty words to me when im walking to the shop, and i must admit i get a little scared, but its alright

marco excused himself saying he needed the toilet, and through the window two minutes later we heard a gun being cocked and: fuck with her again, wallah ill shoot you all!

1 onion 4 peppers 200ml boiled rice and 200g minced meat
mum called, i said turn off the music, and to the mandem shut up, everyone was silent, she goes hi, where are you, i said at marcos, she said nothing, and then, are you coming home tomorrow, i found Babas recipe when i was having a clearout, stuffed peppers, i can make it for you, i was like, no, ill eat with the boys

you are who you are
marco and i was out with some you know, pretty
religious guys, when we met arjan in town, and he was
with this other guy, you know, brokeback mountain and
that, afterwards people was saying, whos that, and arjan
just froze, uh uh uhhh, but marco stepped in and said,
khalas bro, hes a free man

champ
man was always talented at boxing, ever since i was little watching fights on the pc, shadowboxing in the mirror and that, playfighting, fighting, had a bag in the living room, and the whole time i trained, punches in the gym, training at this spot in helsfyr, always asking the olders a hundred questions, getting answers and asking ten more, the gym got to be home number 2, zero chaos, zero street, zero karni

for a while man wanted to be a pro too, swear down i had a plan get me, a good plan, such a sick feeling, you got no idea, and i often think about that one thing, how sick id be now if id just kept on, i woulda been extreme, the champ by now for sure you get me, Baba would be proud for sure

walalo 1
and the people there was mad, like that one time i met a guy there, it was his first time, the guy was a hundred and fifty kilos of beirut kebab and fries, and i didnt know him, but i said, bro, you just started innit, he goes, yeah, i said, cool, you wanna get some pads and spar a bit, then we trained for like half an hour, and i thought damn, mans got balls coming into a gym like a hundred and fifty kilos and like, yeah, let me try boxing, when he aint never done it before

the gym
last week me and the boys was on a round of amy, and
someway somehow we ended up on the same street as
the gym, and its time since i been there, it was almost
like i forgot it was there, cos we was standing there
snorting powder and i didnt clock where we was before
it was too late, but all of a sudden one of them older
hard man who used to train me was coming along down
towards us, and bro, my heart bounced a thousand
floors, swear down, racing like it was olympic games or
some shit, like yalla, bringing the gold home bringing
the gold home, i prayed to god my man wouldnt check
me, sweaty and thin with my nose white like some filthy
fucking junkie

arjan panting, marco like, why we running,
you know him?

walalo 2
and the other day i went gym again, mustve been a year since last time, and my brother from back in the day was there, the one i sparred with when he was a hundred and fifty kilos, and swear down, i almost didnt recognise man, cos this brothers lost so much, like sixty-five kilos!! sixty-five kilos, imagine, my man dropped a whole filipino, one whole bredda stripped off his belly innit, practically got rid of a moped, a little motorbike, you get me

after we caught up hes like, cuz, lets spar a bit like last time, i said, sure, we went into the ring, i had to borrow some gloves from there, but fam! we went one round, break, started another one, i had to say cuz, k-k-khalas, stop, he goes, what you mean stop, we aint done, i say, brother im done, he said, done, what you mean done, i was breathing heavy, he said: ivor, you lost it or what, what happened to you?

mr vigeland
marco got a girl and at the end they was wiling out so much man was taking it out on us so today were in vigeland park and jonas points, like marco thats you, and marcos like what and turns round

it was that statue of a fat angry baby

sports injuries 1
i miss training, i just feel like everythings better then, and the mandem aint training either, marco used to play football before, he was real good too, but like jonas for example, hes never done sport, we asked, and he just went, was in the choir once, does that count?

and sure, arjan played football, but i dont know what happened there cos now he hates it still, we was gonna meet and we was by the football pitches, like yalla, come here, he just went, no, we said, come on, he was like, nah fuck that shit

jonas grandma 2
marco found out some guys that owed him money was at a shubz somewhere, so we headed over, me, him, arjan and jonas rocked up like we was about to harvest some bamboo, and when we sent the rest of the party out, the people who owed money heard marcos voice from the hallway and two of them jumped down off the veranda, it was the kind with two floors, but this other man didnt have the balls, so marco dragged him into the living room, sat him on the floor and started talking, and personally if four man with machetes was standing over me in an empty yard, id be getting out that floos, but this man here was refusing to listen and in the end we flipped and started shouting, and im thinking the neighbours gonna ring the feds soon and well get caught, but then jonas phone rings, and he shouts, its my grandma, i gotta take it! and everyone goes silent, even my man on the floor, and maybe it was something to do with marco holding a machete to his neck, but anyway no one said a word until jonas was like: love you too, take care

304s never change 1
after a short and dramatic journey marcos single again, we was sitting in istanbul in grønland eating this fantastic lahmacun, when marco got added by this guy on snap whos like, your girl? 🌀🌀🌀 and sent this video that was not chill at all, cos in the video this girls in the disabled toilets at burger king getting banged by three guys

304s never change 2
marco goes fuck them man still, the winner has the last laugh wallah, ill show them

overnight delivery
when marco freaks, he either goes norwegian dictionary or full somali, and this time was his mother tongue, so the only thing i got was little words here and there, like traitor whore fuck love and im hungry what should we eat after, luckily this guy i was shotting to was somali so he translated, sounds like your friend needs more than food wallah, anger management express

ingrid

we was sitting in beirut after bunning some green direct from amster and a bit of gina direct from tøyen, and it was late in the day, eight for sure, but outside the sky was still light with late summer sun, and we was munching like we never seen food before, and all of a sudden jonas goes, reckon you can ask the king for ingrid alexandras snap, i was just like, bro, what you mean the king, if you want her snap you just gotta reach a shubz shes at, and arjan goes, yeah, and grow twenty centimetres and some balls, but marco sighed, he said, no brothers please, dont give the boy hope, and he laughed, and jonas fullllly freaked, shaking from head to toe and trying to say something, when arjan jumped in like, anyway if anyones catching her its me, and marco just shook his head, no way theyre letting an indian in the palace, are you mad, and arjan went, yeah, they need one for diversity, youre black, they already filled that quota

alexandra
i gave it a shot and said, most probably it would be me
whod catch her, but marco shut that shit down straight
off and said, number one russia invaded ukraine, theyre
never letting you in, and number two youre polish, only
way youre getting in the palace is to clean the bathroom

the notebook, traphouse edition
but i aint that kind, burger king disabled toilets and
all that shit, jumping from ting to ting like it was a
trampoline park no way, swear down, mans a romantic

real talk
what i really want is to catch a wifey

studying law 2
at lunch today that teacher from law came took me aside, she said, hey ivor, hows it going, good, and she goes are you sure? you can tell me if somethings wrong, and i thought, wagwan? this gyal become a psychologist or what? but she went on like, yeah, cos things were going so well to begin with, and now you havent handed in anything in a long time, she said, i know it can be a lot, im here if you need anything

bomb shelter
we copped 3g of molly and 2 of speed between us and jonas got so parro we died, my man like, yo we better watch out we better watch out cos wed skipped school, every time a car came along, jonas ran off the pavement and behind a building, and since we was in the middle of town and it was the middle of the day, it happened quite a lot, like the whole time, and after a bit the acid kicked in too, and since the tabs were old wed taken two each, and just when they exploded in us, the air raid sirens went off cos it was testing day, so then i preed marco who was preeing me who was preeing arjan who was preeing the trees, and we all knew it was once in a lifetime and what we needed to do, so when jonas started like, hear that, hear that?? the russians are coming!! we was just like, bro, hear what, its completely silent, and in the end he started screaming and ran off to find a bomb shelter

catch a case
it was night before i reached home, and on the way a junkie was walking in front of me, and man was walking slow and crooked and all over the place and looking confused in general, and in the end he stopped, stood there, swayed and fell over, faceplanted right on

the tarmac, couldnt even put out his hands, i rolled him over, he was lying there gurgling on the street, blood coming from his nose and his cheek all scraped up so his whole fucking face was covered with a mix of blood, spit, mud and snot, and in the back of his throat he was making these fucked noises that made me feel sick, and his eyes was empty and glazed, it was like his soul had ghosted and never come back, and i called 113, and when i saw the ambulance had spotted us, i bounced, cos if they feel like it, the feds will come and youll catch a case

childrens services
we all have different case workers at childrens services, or before jonas and i had the same one, but then they found out we was bredren and gave him a new one, he was like, fuck them yeah, the last one was decent, but even if we got different idiots, swear down all of them are trying the same thing, which is to split us up

marcos case worker, mine, arjans and now this new one jonas got, they all chat the same bullshit, heyyy you gotta get away from them boys, theyre no good for you, we have to take action, maybe move you somewhere, you cant hang with them no more

always the same stories, again and again, them man are parrots swear down, and they think were fucking each other up, but they dont get its the other way round, we woulda been getting high anyway, we the ones looking out

young radicals
when we discuss religion in public places like cafes
restaurants metro, even marco lowers his voice and
looks over his shoulder cos he says if these whiteys here
hear too much, swear down them fascists gonna get all
the votes

304s never change 3
since the video situation with his ex marcos had two goals, bang every (?) shorty in oslo and post pictures to stories every time, and set up at least one of the man from the video

today we sorted one of them tings, and let me tell you, mans heartbreak is almost cured

tu casa es mi casa (y tus airpods, también son míos)
last week there was a wave of robberies in town, and
so on monday i had new airpods phone and gucci
belt, but also my whole double period social studies
was about youth crime and repeat offenders, and the
teacher theres all idealist free soul marriage-is-a-prison
etc, only now shes standing there talking about the
bad consequences of the same things shes normally
pushing, like for example, these young people lack male
role models and are drawn to older men on the street,
and the class nodded like oh thats so interesting, while
im sitting there texting marco, cos wed already talked
about this a thousand times, and in the end she said,
what these children actually need is someone who can
check in with them every day, help them set goals, open
them up, teach them about discipline, help them get
in touch with their emotions blah blah blah, and you
know, the bitchs glowing like she invented the wheel,
so i stood up and clapped like: congratulations, thats
called a dad

sports injuries 2
me and arjan had a competition who can take the most gina without passing out and we both ended up puking and after marco rocked up and we took some mandy and one of them man not gonna say who started chatting about when he was little playing football and every friday after training theyd munch pizza drink soda popcorn check a film and after the film everyone left except him cos he had to stay and help the trainer tidy up

1692
i swear down some females are flipping out, today i walked out of school cos it was the end of the day and i seen two gyal running down towards the station even though there was no train and after them was like fifteen other gyal with phones out filming, shouting, fucking ho fucking slut ill kill you myself and suddenly them first two are in the station with nowhere to run, and them other gyal made a big circle round them like modern day witch trials, and i swear no fucking around, these bitches start spitting at them, not a little bit either no no like theyre having a competition, and all the while theyre filming and shouting loose evil skinny skint fat fake ho slut, and in the end the boss gyal grabs the hair of that one wretch and pulls her right to the edge of the platform, she goes, you chat to my man again and ill throw you in front of the train wallah

wearing the trousers
and i told marco, he was like, forget whos wearing the trousers, that bitchll give you a wedgie so hard itll cut you in two

304s never change 4
we tumbled into this mad shubz up in holmen, but guess what we tumbled out again just as quick cos marcos ex was there and her new man too, and seems like marcos heartbreak aint as cured as we thought, cos the second he seen her, he freaked, like, you ho sket fuckin slut ilaahe ha ku baabiiyo etc etc, and then her man, who we still didnt know was her man, he freaks out too, like who you talking to, speak norwegian la la la, thats my girlfriend, but when he said it, marco stopped screaming and started cracking up, and the whole place was silent while marco was getting it together and my man was getting redder, and in the end marco pulls out his phone and puts on the video, he goes, this your gyal wallah, public toilet of fucking oslo man

the diplomats
today we was sitting in maccie ds when this older guy like maybe 24 comes over to us and goes, are you marco and ivor? were like yeah whos asking, he goes you know that man from there, yeah, he says you lot pulled one, he says youd better ring and say sorry before tomorrow, he says if you dont ring, youre fucked, he says if you dont ring, youre gonna die

and then this guy leaned towards us, like dropped his voice and got into some godfather psychosis shit, goes, and boys, you know he dont fuck about, you know its gonna be chaos

marco goes, ok, was that all? and before my man could say shit marco shouts, great, so tell that motherfucker he can suck my fat nigga dick

photo album
some things you dont tell no one, like how you dont like photo albums, and if mum gets it out, you leave, cos if you dont you get a bad feeling in your guts and feel hot, cos like, she aint here no more

jonas grandma 3

we was at jonas grandmas cos she was making waffles, and then we played yahtzee, and one time jonas won, and he was really happy, and actually no one wanted to leave, cos when youre at jonas grandmas it feels a bit like being a kid again, but we had no choice cos me and marco had to go cop another bar, arjan had childrens services and jonas had to go home, but before we bounced, we had to wash up, and me and arjan was fucking about a bit, so in the end marco freaked, like she let you in her home and you cant even fucking tidy up, fucks wrong with you lot

re.eu
i wont say who, but this friend of mine dont fuck regular bitches no more, so now its all realescort, eight bags a month for sure on realescort, black, white, yellow, blindfold, he dont discriminate, but yesterday there was this massive report in the paper or some shit about the feds catching pimps, and now theyre gonna catch the johns too cos all them man paid on their phones with vipps innit, so first im thinking, good job man landed on drugs not chicks, but then i showed the article to my brother, like, what you saying, you fucked or what, and he read like three lines before he saw the word vipps and went off on me like never before, like, owww you think im a fucking retard or you think im dumb enough to use vipps on whores? you ok do i look like a fool do i look like i was dropped on my head when i was little wheres the scar blah blah blah, and he must have carried on for like twelve minutes before he picked up airpods sour face and a snus, and apparently i got this massive silent treatment cos i was dumb enough to ask, but we was at the kebab shop in majorstuen and theres a mirror on the wall there, so when he got out his phone i looked in the mirror and he was googling how to close your vipps account

young and promising
some man from middle school was in the central
station under the sign there, so we stopped, fucked
around with them a bit, smoked some chips, chatted
shit, created a little chaos and that, marco had some
mad diss back and forth with this one kid, in the end
the kid pushed it and marco smacked him up

and jonas was pranging g you already know, the boys
always shaking like a fucking leaf when theres so many
man, especially them roadman, you know them man are
chaos, or well, us, them, same difference

afterwards i reached narvesen to get more packs of
chips and was chirpsing the chick at the till, albanian or
some shit, but as i was coming back, two people passed
by me, thirty years old maybe, proper straight, like play
nice people you know, they probably have wine tastings
and talk about how many foreigners you could fit on a
cruise ship, anyway they gave marco and the boys such
a look, you know like when you go petrol station toilet
and the whole shit stinks like its never been cleaned,
thats how they checked marco, and then one of them
opened her mouth, my god this bitch was chatting so
loud like she had tinnitus or some shit, she was just like

yeah, are they these new gangs you think, and then she clicked her tongue against her teeth like this tsk tsk, and the other ones voice was just as fucked up, she was like, yeah, its the next generation, theyre even worse, i saw it on the news

seen
crazy people, those bitches, probably aint never spoken
to man before, just seen pictures on the news of some
guy getting arrested, hes wearing a puffa, afterwards she
think every man whos not cold is a criminal

swear down if you was gonna judge her after one look,
lotta man woulda said she eats too many big macs

halloween
this weekend it was halloween and we must have
robbed like fifteen guys stuff, phones airpods hash
chips cash we aint fussy, just bouncing from shubz to
shubz, jacking people and moving on, and no one knew
shit cos we had scream masks and deep voices, and we
ended up in some shubz in town snorting molly and
snow until our noses was dripping blood

1-2-3
and i said to marco high grade was no good for him cos
if my man has three brain cells sober when hes high he
only has two, then he said to me that winters not good
for me cos if i was pale before im a ghost now

we took the metro to grønland and took a seat in brown bar where they dont id and bought beer and shots of gammel dansk, and arjan said he knew why it was called brown bar, and we said thats not why, and in the bag was a shelf stackers monthly salary in powder form, and plan was for it to be gone by sunrise

we sat on these tall chairs in the window by the door, and on the tv they had german football that people was cheering even though they was norwegian, man was sending snaps, need 1g, 2g, as well as a couple who wanted 5 or 10, and then i sent arjan off on a voi scooter to where they was

before we left id put up a story
top snow in right now ❄ ❄
1 1000
3 2800
5 4500
free delivery on 5+
hmu 📱 online till 4am

pipervika
today we was in pipervika cos even if its autumn, the sun paid a little visit, and plus we got moncler, hoods, mdma and scarves, so all in all it was actually a very nice day with all the options, but yesterday marco copped the goods for me like usual, and the rule no exceptions is hes gotta go straight and reach the shorty i stash with, but he decided to stop and have a joint, and maybe someone smelled it cos suddenly the feds was everywhere, and marco took off and had to dash the bag, and in the end he sprinted through the forest up to the blocks and climbed up on a balcony on the second floor, and he sat there with sweaty palms and visions of lockup while he checked bare feds running round beneath him, and when he finally climbed down and went back the bag was gone

and thats why today me and marco buss up like never before, and jonas sat right on the end of the pier hands over ears while arjan lay on the edge half asleep on shrooms, and i was so angry i screamed at marco, aint you never heard of dont shit where you eat, and then he got up in my face so i could smell his booze breath and see every little beard hair and scar, and in the air this mad current, you coulda charged a tesla still, and he yelled at me, what about you, aint you never learned dont get high on your own supply, and one maybe two seconds later i thought, if i throw him off the pier will anyone see cos marco cant swim, but then arjan opened his eyes like, owwww burn, and all i could do was laugh

right?
it was autumn outside and cold so we sat in the deepest
corner of beirut, and all the boys had kingkong with
extra fries and meat and on the side a falafel plate to
share and drinks of course, and the place was chill cos
it was evening, and wed pulled two tables together,
and i put the floos on top while all the man counted in
whispers even though wed already counted on the train,
and it was 13 thousand krone notes 47 five hundred
notes 9 two hundred and 7 hundred, and the table was
purple blue and yellow like the worlds most beautiful
flag, and my body was itching and my legs trembling,
and i knew i knew, that now were here, now ive done
it, no one can stop me, over, done

mashallah, whispered marco, cold kebab never again,
said arjan, no more used snus, said jonas, no way back,
i thought

police

two endz was gonna have a clash in the forest outside town, there was a lot of people there, musta been a hundred man in trackies and shiny puffas, looked like some reverse kkk meeting swear down, and mans getting gassed while all we was waiting for was the crew from the other endz to rock up, and some man said, dun know they pussied out wallah, bitches for real, but then some other man went, nah, theyre coming up from the bus, and so anyway everyone was mad hyped and got their phones ready to film and put up stories and shit its going off 💥 💥 💡 and man gonna get fucked up today 🔫 🔫

me, jonas and arjan was already there, but marco was late as per cos he bunned a zoot after dinner and fell asleep, so we laid into him in the chat, like, ohhh marco cant even handle watching a clash, and he freaked a bit, and i thought thats why he called jonas, but no, jonas was like, ivor, talk to marco yo, i think hes had that bad kief theyre always chatting about, and i said why, he just goes, cos hes saying oskars coming, we better run, and me and arjan laughed, what you mean oskars coming? i dont know no oskar, so i said to jonas, ask what marco means, a few seconds passed, jonas went he just says oskars coming, theres shirts in the forest, and we laughed and laughed and laughed some more, right up until arjan pointed at some black shapes coming down the slope with dogs and handcuffs, and we clocked that shirts meant shurta, oskar meant askar, and we better run

khanzir
on the way down the stairs to the metro in grønland
the feds came along, like, ivor, marco, stop a moment,
and they asked if wed been in the forest for a clash
last weekend and where were we off to now and did
we have anything on us, and we said no to everything,
but still they was like, ok, wed better check, and in my
head i was thinking, why do you ask if youre gonna do
it anyway and when is that receipt ticket thing gonna
start, but anyway one of the feds tried to get hold of
marco, but marcos like, get off, i cant touch pigs, its
haram, and i was bussing with laughter even though
my face was against the wall and bars and shank in
my pocket, and marco carried on with the jokes, and
next week theres gonna be a meeting with the feds and
maybe well get a fine

you can come over here
anyway they didnt do no paedo shit that time, its so
weak man you dont know, fucking strip off your clothes
in front of some grown man, squat and cough, the fuck?

dad
in little school when we got assignments to write
about your family, write about your childhood, i always
tried to make up stories and lie, better that than the
shortest presentation in the class, like, dead, locked up,
dunno, dunno

hot shot
yesterday we told jonas what a hot shot is, just to fuck with him a little, like, you never know with these man here bro, one day you might wake up with a needle in your arm, or maybe you wont wake up, but jonas still wasnt shook, he just got gassed, like aaayyyyiiii, this is the smartest way to buss man up, when we gonna do it, who we gonna hit, and then he went completely alex jones on us like, you reckon that man there got hit with a hot shot, what about that man, or her, and basically he went through everyone we know who died of an overdose

the art of dying
and after that he was like, must be the best way of dying, overdosing yeah, maybe mans going hell, but at least well die in heaven still

how much death we gotta see before we get to live
and the other day i met a junkie we know, he told me
about this brother who died, a brother me and marco
used to roll with when we was little, twelve, thirteen or
whatever, he was always strict with us, never gave man
shit, like juice or chips even, just a wagging finger and
that whole stay-in-school business, and he watched out
for us against them age-aint-nothin-but-a-number guys

i came over all emotional you get me, and this junkie
says, he goes, you might love the streets, but theyre
never gonna love you back, afterwards i told marco, he
was just like, shit yo, mans never getting used to this eh

dance you pussy
some man jacked marcos watch at a shubz when he was in the pool and no one wanted to say who, but now two weeks later some next man sends me a snap, like check this story, mans selling a watch like marcos, so i grab the contact from the other snap, but this mans saying, no meetings only mail, payment first, i thought fine and gave his snap to this one gyal, and then the other, and after a week of chatting, pictures, facetime, the works, they agreed to meet up one night by a preschool near where he lives

i reckon man was a little surprised when he saw me and marco on that bench and not some petite little lightskinned ting with a nice round booty and curly hair, marco was like, lets go 1-on-1, then he banged man up and filmed it on his phone, it was dark, he had the torch on, like, kiss my shoes, do burpees, ten, five, twenty, tell me youre my bitch, he put it up on a private story, then we followed the guy home, took the watch and that, marco smashed up his tv, the ladies got 1500 each

helen keller 1
marco called, cos after me and arjan took mandy
yesterday things didnt go so well, so now arjans in the
hospital cos hes blind as helen keller, and i went blind
once too, but with him it didnt get better, so after he
fell down the stairs, the home called 113 and made
a scene, and i dont feel so great either cos my livers
singing its final verse like its diseased and its chronic

so now im lying on the bathroom floor cos standing ups
not an option, but marcos coming by with a little speed
later so its gonna be alright, i called him real quick,
guy was like, awwww bro this aint cool g, you gotta go
hospital. i said, no

helen keller 2 (the passport)
after the helen keller episode last week the home
decided to put arjan on piss tests

and seems like arjan wasnt really feeling it, cos when
the home said to him, since you dont have any other id,
you need to take your passport along the first time you
go, he said aight bet and dashed his passport in the river

skinny dipping and mdma
we was at a shubz at this rich gyals mansion with a sauna and massive garden, and since it was winter and there was snow on slopes and noses, we decided to get naked in the snow, but on the way out marco shouts to this gyal, yo wait! and she was like what is iiiiit, and then he says in this mad stern voice, watch the whitey, wallah hes got zero pigment, you lose him in the snow, we might never see him again

christmas eve
its christmas eve and man shoulda actually been doing some other shit, mum was like, cant you stay at home for once, but christmas aint for me, and jonas pops is away and his flats empty, so since marco dont celebrate and arjans gonna be eating meatballs with two support workers, i said fuck it, lets cotch

we met at the mall right by jonas place, and he even had on a red christmas jumper with bare tiny rudolphs on it, and he was mad gassed and laughing his high little laugh the whole time cos he aint celebrated proper christmas for ages, and even arjan seemed happy for once, he was wearing a white shirt and had done his hair with like two bottles of hair gel and olive oil

first we ducked into the shop to get food, real family and that, and after five or ten minutes we was out again, but jonas was nowhere to be seen, and another ten minutes passed, and we was sure he got grabbed, and we started planning how we was gonna do reverse prison break in the back room, but then out of the massive sliding doors comes this little guy in an enormous winter coat, and with one hand hes pulling one of them shopping baskets on wheels full of booze, but in the other is this enormous white package almost bigger than him, and with this huge grin he lifts the package over his head like its simba the lion cub and shouts out so any man can hear, ay look man i jacked a spare rib!!

helen keller 3 (the book)
during christmas dinner we was chatting about arjan throwing away his passport, and he went, yeah marco, now theres two of us who aint got the little red book, you aint alone no more, and marco was like you fucking hubba bubba, wallah koran im a norwegian citizen, and arjan was like, lets see your book then, and marco said fool, i aint brought my passport to christmas lunch, and then arjan banged his fist on the table like a judge with a hammer and shouted, case closed, marco never had a passport

Jesus birth and the old ladys death (almost)
and arjans mum overdosed christmas day
he heard a crash in the kitchen and found her on
the floor
shes in the hospital

helen keller 4 (mike tyson)
arjan came into beirut after his passport appointment, and i dont know how they got an appointment so quick cos the whole of norways waiting, but anyway this indian brother got an appointment in four days, and when he came in, he had this massive tattoo on his face looking like mike tyson, so we was like awww, arjans lost it, but no the brother just smiled, went bathroom and came back with the tattoo half gone, we was like, whats going on, indian carnival or some shit, and he just grinned, like, you lot know the passport aint gonna be valid if its with a tattoo i aint got, and we laughed, we said, you sure about that, and he went, pretty sure, and then we went back and forth for like ten minutes, so i dunno, well see if arjan gets another week without piss tests or if hell have to go round with this dumb nitty passport till hes twenty-five

helen keller 5 (positive)
so arjans plan didnt work cos the home baited his ting and grabbed the passport in the post, and when they saw mans photo theyd clearly had enough and said, aight you wanna be the indian mike tyson, be my guest, you aint getting another appointment, so now jonas is the only one not on piss tests, and arjan already had his first test, and its definitely gonna be positive, but also he posted a picture of the photo to his stories and like a hundred man screenshotted and posted it in theirs, cos a charged indian with red eyes and a fake mike tyson face tat gotta be the sickest passport photo in norwegian history

what doesnt kill you . . .
and when i was little, i thought i had the coolest background on my phone, it was this picture of mike tyson with the words what doesnt kill you makes you stronger, and i had an iphone 3gs with true skate and jetpack joyride, and in the morning i ran so fast to school to find marco and show him my sick new background, and he came over and i was like look look look, and he looked at the phone for like two seconds then stared up at me with this resigned grownup face and went, bro, if you get smashed up by a bus after school, are you stronger or just a vegetable? dumb background wallahi

voldemort
and just after christmas i found myself in a little fight with a bunch of guys, i got pepper sprayed first, then banged in the face so fucking hard it almost sent me flying, i swung my shank in the air full blind and something hit and some man screamed, and after i met the mandem, marco was like look at this boy lol, voldemorts in oslo fam

journey to the christmas star 1
jonas got badded up in town again, basically we was
on the way to the metro to cop a little molly, when
suddenly i heard jonas yelling, i h-h-havent done
anything! and i turn and see his face getting caved in
by fists in this mad slow motion, then ok he ran, with
like seven, eight older guys after him down the road, so
then i ran up to him too, and i thought this gonna be
fine cos theres a lot of us man too, me, marco, arjan and
a few breddas from middle school, but all of a sudden
were standing in the road, i turn around, boom, aint
no man there

so me and jonas are surrounded by eight wasteman,
theyre shouting and that, pulling off their belts,
throwing bottles at us, im thinking aight, guess well
be taking a beating, but im definitely gonna catch one
man first, so i knock down this one man and enjoy it
for like two and a half seconds before its my turn, and
suddenly im on the ground with punches raining, boom
boom boom im seeing stars, orions belt you get me,
journey to the christmas star and whatnot, im hearing
hanne krogh whisper my name and i know were done
for, finito, these man gonna put me in a coma, ok ivor,
this is the end, but suddenly i hear this loud yell, honest

to god battle cry, i look up, eyes drenched in blood, and there they are, arjan and marco sprinting down road towards us, dashing stones and chairs like theyre on the palestinian frontlines

journey to the christmas star 2
man cant carry that many chairs and stones at once, so when the boys was empty and all them man was still standing around, arjan shouted ima shoot you, ima shoot you, and waved an airsoft gun around, then they all took off

and you know brother, it was on this day i really started digging arjan cos i seen a lot of man run when it goes off, but this man here, true brother still, people can send who they want for man, kgb, fbi, pst, na, fuck it, send em all, well still be standing shoulder to shoulder

THE FALL

helen keller 6 (identity theft)

oh yeah, so when arjan posted that photo of his passport, of course he posted the whole thing and never crossed nothing out, cos like why not, so today i got a snap off some guy whod bought a passport pack on the dark web and got arjans, so i told arjan, who told the home, and since his passport leaked, hes gotta get a new one

the leg
these older guys who always grab from me invited us to a shubz, so we was with them in this flat in bjørvika, and the whole night snapsnapsnap, the samsungs going bananas, i went myself, or if it was someone we knew, i sent arjan

this new man calls, and i reached to meet him, marco came out cos he wanted to bunn a zoot anyway, it was all as per, they wanted a two, i waited behind the brown brick buildings by the lake, and marco stood by the water blazing

i recognised them too late, it happened so quickly i never realised until i was waking up and staring at the sky, head banging body not working like normal, my left leg warm, throbbing, like my heart was in there and not in my chest, marco was standing over me on the phone, arjan and jonas came sprinting over the snow, marco looked different, shook, even if he was laughing too, laughing like he was hysterical, with eyes wide open and all his teeth visible, he said, ivor, youre bleeding g, i said, what, but his breathing was too fast, he had to lean against the wall, he said, ivor, you got wet up, he said, congratulations on your street confirmation

thats the last time youre coming round here
marcos always watching war films on hbo so he said to arjan
and jonas, hold him down, and ivor, bite on something,
in the end it was my gucci wallet, then he poured vodka
on the gash and really took charge, sent arjan to central
station to sort out a bandage and some big plasters at the
pharmacy, and jonas to tøyen for more booze, marco sat
next to me and just, bro you gotta chug, wallahi, doctors
orders, cos if not youre gonna get mad pain once the
adrenalines gone, so i chugged, then arjan and jonas went
together to the station, while me and marco got picked up
by this man marco knows who drove us to marcos yard

like five minutes before we got there, i got mad dizzy, and
when i was getting out of the car, i was so wiped, marco
was serious, shook, he said, ivor, we gotta go hospital, we
gotta gotta gotta, i said, marco, no, then we got into it a bit,
or i was mostly shaking my head cos my breath was going
like id raced up a mountain, we was in his room, they was
carrying me in, blood everywhere, outside, entranceway,
stairs, the hallway in his flat, i was lying on the floor, it was
dark, drifting, head heavy, from the living room i heard
marco and his mum arguing in somali, i understood a word
here and there, he said mum, we aint got nowhere to go,
in the end she shouted haye! ok, but tani waa markii ugu
dambeysay ee aad halkan timaadovi

a tradition is made
a little later i asked marco about them street
confirmation things cos id never heard no one say that
and thought maybe it came from some tv show or 1930s
mafia documentary cos marco watches a lot of films like
that and thinks he gets brownie points, but marco was
like no, when he saw me on the ground and preed the
blood, man got in a total panic so he did what we all do
when things get too mad, and thats saying some stupid
shit and hoping some man laughs

all thats missing is weddings and funerals
so after marco came up with street confirmations he
thinks hes clever or some shit cos yesterday we was
in town chugging and i was pretty gone so marco
pushed me in the fountain at the national museum like,
congratulations wallahi now you been christened too

ungraded
one of the vaterland alkies we hung with said once, the school of life aint the way to go, you drop out here you drop out for good

young dumb love
but all that madness made me hungry, you get me, it
made me obsessed, im gonna do big things, everyones
gonna know who i am, everyones gonna know i got
it, if you was at preschool with me 1 day you gonna
know who i am, when youre eating dinner with pasta,
parmesan and fake friends, you gonna say yeah, but you
know what, i actually know him, we was at preschool
together, the fact you walked past me once ten years
ago gonna be your party trick
hungry, you get me?

and it works and all, thats the best thing, like a while
back i met this chick from little school, and she was
talking to me different, god knows, cos now she knows
who i am, that im bringing in the ps, fixing shit, she
was like, its so weird to think of you that way, after she
was talking with this like, whats the word, they say it in
books and shit, wait yeah

yeah: awe

deli 1
every day i go past deli de luca on grønland torg, and every time i look in like fuck them motherfuckers, charging a hundred and seven kroner for snus yo, tryna rob me and that, wtf?
but today i went in cos behind the counter was this chick, and bro, my heart woke up, get me, like yo, hallelujah!
she was tall, an arab, beautiful, big smile, so i went in, spent much too much cash on snus, paying with a thousand krone note, she took her time counting, but i think she was feeling me a little, and you know the ladies sometimes get a little shook then, not like me yeah, i never get shook, after that i text marco, i said, is it possible to fall in love in three minutes, before he answered i text again, i wrote, i think so

deli 2
ive been thinking a lot about that arab gyal in grønland, why didnt i grab her digits, i really gotta reach get them digits, she was maybe twenty-three, twenty-four, proper grownup lady, i could see that, in her eyes there was like, zero bullshit, so i reached there again, proper simp still, walking past, acting all innocent, but i was actually looking in, hoping she was there, but she wasnt for days,

i was thinking yo, maybe she quit, maybe ima become
a rapper, make a heartbreak album, but then today i
stepped past and boom there she was, i copped a little
snus, started feeling hot, paid cash, she was struggling
this time too, i said to her, countings hard right, your
middle school teacher couldnt find the classroom, she
was just like, hahaha nah, im actually good at maths, she
said, had to do pharmaceutical maths for uni

deli 3
still aint asked for her digits, taking it slow,
dont wanna fuck it up, but anyway shes a dentist, or she
will be, meanwhile shes working part time in the deli
and comes from somewhere outside town, chill lady,
aint been passed around and that, none of the boys
heard of her
good sign
i said to her, whats your name,
she said, ayla, and you
i said tony, see ya
she smiled and went, yeah, see ya

deli 4
aahhh bro, whyd you say your name was tony, dunno,
man, it wasnt planned, just happened, cos i dont know

if shed be feeling me so much if she heard about me
first, get me? so numero uno im gonna let the gyal
get to know me, form her own opinion, and after that
maybe she aint gonna think so much about all them
other things get me?

cos if i was just like, yeah, my names ivor la la la, maybe
shell say to her mate, i met this guy, his names ivor, and
her mates like dont you know who that is? he done this,
he done that, after that she rings the security services,
they stuff a microphone in her hair, like oh, ask him
what happened in the forest
theres not a lot of ivors in oslo still
if my name was abdi no one would know shit, must be
a million abdis here, in middle school we was like abdi
one abdi two abdi three
gotta have a system, get me
and we got up to like thirty or something
but im serious about this ting here bro
for real

helen keller 7 (hat trick)
after arjans passport got spread around the dark web
we thought he was gonna get out of the piss tests cos
he had to grab a new passport, but since hed already
brought it along once, seems he didnt need to wait for a
new one, so today he was there for the second time, and
ive never met a brother who gives less of a fuck about
them tests, he came to beirut right after with a little
baggie of amy and the biggest grin like, two for two,
boys, one more and its a hat trick

ransom

so mans in the deli buying a raspberry water, shes like why you always buy these fruity things, you think youre healthy?

after that we talked for a bit, maybe thirty minutes, and i said ok let me pay, but then i realised id forgotten the ps, swear down it must be the first time since little school i aint had no ps on me, i thought fucks going on eh, and i said, you take vipps, she was like no, so i said fine, but youve got vipps let me vipps you, she was like, hahaha youre trying to be sneaky, i get that youre asking for my number, i said that wasnt the plan, its not all about you, after that i called jonas cos i aint got vipps myself, said, vipps forty kroner to this number here, he was like, ayla, who dat? you in trouble, is this a ransom, i was like what you mean ransom habibi, forty kroner gonna get me out of what, a gym locker?

date
i got her number off jonas, he was like, oooh, ivors in l-l-
love, i said chill b, she took it on the second ring, her voice
so calm, not like in the deli, now she was almost whispering,
hello, who is it? me, who else, i said, you working, when
you done, eight oclock, good, lets get a bite to eat, she
said, hmmm ok, where, i said, ill text you, ill sort it

and its not only important that theres a table free, and
piff munch and that, but its also gotta be somewhere
no other mandem be hanging, so we aint sitting there
chewing pizza chatting sweet love and bam five pakis with
machetes jump out of the bushes, and in the summer
when we was little, we always hung in tjuvholmen,
bunning and grabbing ice cream tubs from movenpick
and walking past new delhi and saying one day wallahi
ima take the finest shorty there and make her my wifey,
so i called and said, hello do you have a table for two this
evening, they was like, no, fully booked, but luckily the
friend of the sister of one of marcos tings works there so
she sorted us a table and marco sent a snap, he said, which
name? i said just choose one, five minutes later hes like,
fine, erik abdullahi, i sent ayla a snap, meet at the national
museum, she replied ok, smiley face, after that half an
hour passed, she wrote, is this the d-word, i wrote yeah

round 1
the food came, and then we talked, but she didnt eat
that much, is that what some chicks do, not eating on
a date cos theyre delicate or some shit, as if i care if you
taste of chicken or cheese, i said to her, you better eat
up, so when we kiss i can have naan bread round 2

round 2
afterwards when we was sitting in the restaurant,
i leaned across the table and showed what an
angry marco would have called total disregard for
consequences, i was like, i didnt bring you here for
chicken and rice, youve got a job to do, and then i
picked up my bag off the floor and said, theres two kilos
of cocaine in here, youre going to take it home, put it
under your bed, and when you get the order, youll get
on a plane to denmark with the bag, when youre back
youll get your money

not a tactical move bro, first she got scared or whatever,
started crying, i was just like hey hey, khalas, just
messing, which was true, in the bag there was just a big
bottle of solo super on special offer and an extra sweater
cos mum said it was cold, and i laughed, but she didnt,
she was just like, thats not ok, if you do that again, itll

be the last time we speak, after that we bounced, it was dark outside, quiet, we walked under the scaffolding over the bridge, past døgnvill, lofoten, fridays and louise, where we serve up blow at the weekends, after that we stopped by the tram, she got out her phone, about to see when the next one was, i ran my fingers through her hair

to think i kissed a boy four years younger than me, she said

different
i said to marco, this chick heres different bro, i wanna treat her good she aint gonna get hurt like the others, marco just went, bro, maybe she is different, but you aint

birthday
yesterday was my birthday, and i dunno what happened, but lately i cant be fucked with no fuss, so when the boys asked, what you wanna do, i said lets just head out in the morning and do candyflips, it was a cold february morning, minus 8, windy, so we sat at the back of maccie ds in majorstuen hoping for the best, a couple of hours before the molly we took the lucy, and by now we got a pretty good grip on the dosage and flow so it was really a very nice trip, i told marco when ive got enough floos, i wanna bounce to the old country still, buy a farm with horses sheep cows cats dogs and zero signal with the nearest neighbour seventy kilometres in each direction and everywhere you look just big open plains with green grass and white gulls so mans always free and the sheep can play, and after a long time thinking marco was like wallahi, sounds buff, but what about the boys, i said, youre coming too obviously, as long as arjan learns to eat cow

good luck . . . believe in yourself
today shes got an exam, a friend translated, i got up
early and texted her: حظ سعيد بامتحانك يا عزيزتي ثق بنفسك

student halls
she got an A of course, so we was celebrating in her
halls, cooking up some food in the shared kitchen that
smelled of stir fry even after man aired it out all day,
straight up kung fu takeover, afterwards some others
that lived there rocked up, made some munch, said,
what you studying?
hahaha, the people there looked at me like i was a
normal person, like id found some secret world, narnia
and that, big trees with castles and shit, or in a way i
was just more me

becoming a man is more beautiful than becoming a king

we was in vaterland park snorting amy and chugging teefed beers, having the biggest discussion with an alkie, he was just like boys, i know, but its not all gold and green forests, the vanilla life might be dull, but at least you got a soft bed and food on the table, i was like, fuck that, nine to five, mortgage, them poor fucks live little lives, slaving away for what? wife and two kids? the alkie leaned forward, he said, you understand croatian, i nodded, he went, think carefully about this, i didnt understand until it was too late:
postati čovjek, je ljepše nego postati kralj

two druggies walk into a bar
ayla asked, and i explained about overdoses and naloxone, she said to me, thats not good, you know? she said, you should have got help, i answered with a joke, some funny shit cant remember what, but she laughed, went quiet, looked around, thought for a moment, leaned towards me, dropped her voice, she said, ive also taken . . . that hash stuff, she was like, i smoked it once in amsterdam, i didnt feel a thing but it burned my throat

munch
she said, and i dont know if it worked, but afterwards the churros tasted really, really good

stone animals
aylas always asking about stuff she aint sure about in norwegian, like today she said, steindyr, whats that, is it deer who live under stones? i was just like, no it means somethings a little on the dear side, very expensive, she laughed and said, so one day well have steindyr things at home, i smiled, and she was like, a steindyr mattress, but no steindyr in the mattress

thin little lizards
and i also asked, whats your favourite animal, she went, those little ones that can change colour, im thinking what, little like . . . i asked what they was called, she said i dont know, but they live on the beach in italy and also theyre the grandchildren of crocodiles

us
we sat on a bench in front of the opera house talking about marco, she said, was he always like that with girls, i was like, no, it started after year six when a girl broke up with him in front of the whole class on the last day of school, but hes single so he can do what he likes still, she was like, yeah, what about you then, are you single? i paused, like my heart was racing, must have been sweating and all, in the end i was like, no, i dont think so, and she goes hmm, i said what about you, she said quietly, no, i dont think so either, after i was like, so its the two of us then, she was like, yeah, its the two of us, and my body felt warm like worlds luckiest man, but also i got this bitter taste or whatever they say, cos marco said it best, he was like, youre no good for her you know that? i was like, yeah, but i dont think she does

sixty-nine
i sat in the car wit marco and arjan and jonas chugging vodka and ghb, and jonas was driving cos he gotta learn manual, and ayla called and got on speakerphone like, hello ya albi hows it going, i said gooood wallahi i love you, she said, have you been drinking, uhh a little, she laughed and said alright, whats seven times seven then, i said forty-nine, and whats forty-nine plus twenty, habibti thats . . . sixty-nine, and from the back seat marco was like, mmm sixty-nine

marco junior
why aint no one taught marco that condoms can
be more than just water balloons, last week was the
third time in eleven days he vippsed a gyal floos for
the morning after pill, arjan said, soon you gonna be
applying to the arts council for your scholarship, artist
at work, but still he never learns, and today we came
into beirut and marcos sitting there with the realest
expression on his face like some man died, so i asked,
and he just looked up real quick like, no, ima be a dad

priorities
first i was totally sure he was kidding, but then he said, you remember the gyal from this and that shubz, yeah she got pregnant and weve decided not to get an abortion

all i could do was laugh, like a trauma response or some shit, me, jonas, arjan was all lying on the floor, lying there howling, even ali behind the counter and the schizo arab chuckled a little, actually everyone was laughing apart from marco, who just got up like, ivor, this is a serious situation, and i need to know youre going to support me and stand by my side (suddenly this mans gone norwegian teacher on me again, got glasses and mustard stains and a belly and shit), and swear down i wanted to be serious, but it wasnt easy when behind him jonas and arjan was sitting there shaking trying not to laugh, so my breath was coming heavy too, and i said, marco, wasnt that the ting you ghosted cos she had a man, and she said you should die and that she was gonna kill herself, and the guy nodded totally serious, yes, but children bring people together and spread love, and i had no answer to that, but luckily the gyal called and said shed decided to get an abortion cos she saw on the internet pregnancy gives you acne

doctors appointment
gods name i thought my leg would be better by now, but its still fucked, and if i sleep with the window open at night i wake up 5:37 with thigh pain like some old bastard with rheumatic hips, and if i dont move it for a long time when were sitting in beirut, it goes to sleep and wont wake up, and if it dont go to sleep and i walk around, it kills like some mans shooting lightning up and down every step i take, so yesterday marco said, bro, i cant handle seeing you like this, and he bounced to get a little oxy for the pain, and after we talked to kjell ivar who uses a stick and gets called the stick cos he got popped in the knee seven years back and never saw no doctor, and kjell ivar dont know much, but he knows about pain relief, so he said up the oxy to 160 and combo with lyrica 600, marco was like, aight, but ivor, maybe you shoulda went doctor that day, for real they coulda sorted you

nine oclock news
and one of the boys, not saying who, was in town on
a voi when he checked man who stabbed me, so he
jumped off and wetted him xx times and rode off, it was
on the main news

gushing blood
fine it was marco, he called me, like, i shanked him
wallahi i wetted that motherfucker, fuck them man, i
said, my brother marco, my fucking brother

family guys
so marco was at the greengrocers with his old lady, and
he dont often go with her cos theres too much beef
now, but he was like fine, and then the crew of that one
man marco wetted spotted him, and it turned harakat,
luckily marco managed to get his old lady in a taxi,
and they bounced, and i spoke to him after, like come
we get them man, but he went, nah bro, my cousins
already gone sort it, and actually marcos cousins are a
mix of cousins uncles nephews and family friends and
they aint so close, but close or not, somalis dont mess
around when it comes to family

vg.no
when i come home, first thing i done was go on vg.no
and seen this massive black box with big red letters:
shooting in xx
marco called the zanco like, first page man, wallahi we
made it

fireworks
them fed motherfuckers stopped us twice today for no
reason, only thing we did was step around town eating
softserve with tutti frutti extra m&ms and enjoying the
sunshine smoking hash, but no, they had to pull over
search us and ask stupid questions like, oh what are you
doing where are you off to where you been have you
heard anything about the guys who got popped at the
weekend we heard they had beef with some yutes

geir lippestad
swear down i used to read a lot
i read every day, before school, in school, after school,
at night

novels, short stories, poems, school books, true story
i was done with law 1 when i was in year six, man was
gonna be a lawyer you know, went on work shadowing
with geir lippestad, the whole business, mad guy, we ate
lunch at some fancy place with fucking peng food but i
couldnt even enjoy it cos i was sooo stressed about what
was gonna happen when the bill came, cos yknow, i had
zero floos, like, shall i run, wash up? then he paid

but that was before, now im not gonna be a lawyer, or
i dont even know if i can, you know criminal record
and shit, im sure i wouldnt get in anyway, or if i did,
suddenly the judge is gonna recognise me haha, just
like, hey youre standing in the wrong place!

nature or nurture 1
we dropped some mandy and soon everyone was feeling emotional, yknow four cats lying on the sofa in storo furniture warehouse sharing brotherly love and dissing each other about whos disappointed their family the most, in the end i said to the boys, if i have kids, i swear things gonna be different, theyre never gonna grow up in chaos like us, and ima have a proper wifey, get me, a real good lady, and after i said: and boys, ima make sure im ready first, fix things up get me, so my kids inherit a house, a house and not scars

i saw marco was feeling it
arjan was asleep

confirmation camp
while jonas was on house arrest, the rest of us hit some shubz in a hood we used to have beef with after jonas (!) got too fucked and made a madness, but like fuck it, we made brownies and did shots with this gyal who was hosting, and the vibe was mad for real, right up until someone snitched that we was there and five or six of these older wasteman rocked up and all of a sudden the whole crib was a war zone, and if marco hadnt been in the pisser when it went off, we probably woulda been vegetables, but when he heard, he came running into the living room waving the beretta, and them man left

i mostly wanted to lie there and never get up again, warm liquid running down the back of my head and down my forehead making my hair sticky, and i knew if i stood up now, i was gonna puke still, and i probably woulda laid there forever and died of shame if the living room hadnt suddenly filled with shouts that cut into my ears, these real panicked screams like a pig getting slaughtered, and when i opened my eyes, i saw the pig was a little boy and the boy was a proper whitey, and we didnt know him, this yute was the girls little brother and must have come running in from the cellar or the attic, and straight off i realised people thought he was jonas, and for once i was happy jonas was on house arrest, if not it might have been him lying on the floor now with both hands on his stomach and beads of sweat on his forehead, and arjan wiped the blood off his face, spat out a wad, picked up a tooth and crawled over to the kid and said, congratulations bro, you know why, the boy was like, n-n-no, arjan said, cos you just got stabbed, he laughed, now you had your street confirmation

city soundtrack
last weekend marco lost his jacket and airpods when he was drunk, he dont listen to music cos its haram, but hes addicted to audiobooks, so today he was like, mans gotta get new airpods get me, im right in the middle of bridget jones diary, so he pulled on a hood and bandana and when we got on the metro, he went all saabye, got some random norwegian

to catch a predator 1
the streets are the maddest grooming site, someone call chris hansen whats going on, mans like thirty banging fourteen-year-olds in the a-hole and that, some of them man here need castrating i swear, when you clock how them man do shit, you get how fucked up the streets are, theyre using fourteen-year-old chicks for sex and yutes for floos, brainwashing some of the kids here and forcing them to work until they either destroyed or locked up, and then they move to the next, mans acting throwaway with peoples lives, you get me, fuck that, predators are predators g

to catch a predator 2
they took you in this expensive car to a fancy restaurant, real places they take your jacket and shit, say sir this sir that and sniffing the wine like someone ripped one off

next time he said, you need something other than ghetto style, and we reached hugo boss follestad, grabbed a watch, new phone, i remember one time we was in the car and i was staring at a hand holding floos, i said yooo, check it so much floos, he said yeah, just wait till you start selling the serious stuff

ghb
me and the boys was out, then marco and jonas said we gonna bounce but me and arjan stayed in town and met a junkie with gina that we bought, but it was strong cos we fell asleep on the pavement and woke up in hospital beds

the hospital
ayla came to the hospital, god knows who told her, i thought fuck, got so shook you cant imagine, said to the nurse im having a panic attack need a xanax, he was like unfortunately i cant give you that, then i looked around, like where can i hide, where can i run, if i jump three floors, how much will it hurt

im scared
she said, habibi, i want this, but i dont know if i can handle any more, i wish it was just us in another town with none of this around, without oslo, she said, its pulling you away, its pulling you down, ana khayfe ya rohi, i can see you disappearing

deep sleep
after the shubz last night jonas overdid the gina again, we was at max in grønland and he fell asleep, or we thought he was asleep, cos he always falls asleep when hes been chugging, but when we was gonna bounce, he wouldnt wake up, just sat there with his head on the table, breathing weird like some longass meditation, and we shook and clapped and shouted and slapped, but no answer so we called 113, and i just got home maybe three minutes ago, cos we hung there till they said he was ok, and marco said wallahi, im never touching gina again, and me and arjan nodded too like we agreed, even though we all know it aint true and just like me theyre probably gonna take gina to go sleep tonight still

dharbaaxo
arjan called marco, like, yo you know that one man who
jacked jonas yeah, hes in the park right this minute,
so all of a sudden we had to take off and jump on the
metro and soon we was there and arjan took marco over
to where my man was in the forest behind vigelands
monolith while i stood guard, but way too quick this
ting in the worlds shortest skirt spilled beer broken
shoe and big bouncing tits comes stumbling down the
steps like, police police, heeeeelp theyre fighting, and
then i clock id better step up cos marcos just getting
started, and as per the feds are sitting right there just
waiting to grab man like us, so i start running like i was
going some place and crash into one of them khanzir
on the way, and i think it worked, cos even though
me and marco was sitting in cuffs on the grass seven
minutes later, at least marco got grabbed for running
away and not for badding man up, and he was at my
side with the feds right in front so we couldnt chat, but
i was mad curious and i reckon marco clocked cos he
nudged me like: all good wallahi, gave man a dharbaaxo
with the bastoolada, my man opened up like a fucking
garden hose

state of fright
feds come and grabbed mans phone so we hadnt spoken in two days, i called from a new number, she went, is it you? i laughed, like, who else, voice shaking, she said, ive been so scared, i read on tv2 someone got shot, he was sixteen, i said, that wasnt me, and she went, but one day it will be you, how come you dont get that?

sharing is caring
today ayla wasnt answering her phone snap text in the end i reached her place like, whats going on with you, and at first she didnt say nothing, but after she was like: i cant be together with you if you keep doing the things you do

khalas
i was sitting in maccie ds with marco when ayla called, she was crying and said when she was on her way home with a friend two guys stopped them, like, you ivors girl, she went no, they said, dont lie, then one of the guys pulled out a shank and said, watch who you fuck wallahi, i asked what they looked like, and she told me, and i know who they are and where one of them lives so me and marco are on the way there now, i said to her, its gonna be fine, theyre never gonna fuck with you again, no one messes with my girl, she said ivor, i love you but i cant take this anymore
its over

a question of guilt 1
i was fully spinning out i shouted to marco these motherfuckers here aint got no respect going after my woman what the fuck they doing she aint got shit to do with this who the fuck they think they are, marco laid a hand on my shoulder, he said, ivor, we are one hundred per cent gonna take them fools but dont forget if she hadnt been with you, she wouldnt have got fucked with

happy families 2
so marcos parents are married, but seems like their
marriage aint been going too well lately cos on saturday
they woke him up with blueberry pancakes halal bacon
and no lip even though he got home late, and actually
everything was tiptop until the third pancake when
his old lady was like, yeah and by the way were getting
divorced and your dads moving out tomorrow, and then
things wasnt so great no more and the pancakes was
dry and the bacon wasnt as good as the real thing even
though hes never tried it apart from that one time when
we was little staying over somewhere and didnt know
no better, but we wont talk about that still, and an hour
later we was sitting in the net on the pier all four of
us waiting for the molly to kick in as we sipped vodka
and gina, and when it finally hit, marco started crying
and went, what happened to in sickness and in health
wallahi, she think they was chatting bout fever?

white cup
i had a meeting with childrens services yesterday and they said if you dont get yourself together well send you to a home, and then i had to battle myself not to send the dude through the window cos a home, thats the limit, but he said from now on ill have to do piss tests twice a week instead of once, monday and thursday, and not gonna lie, that was smart, monday especially gonna fuck man right up

positive/negative
only decent thing about this new arrangement is that now me and marco got our tests right after each other on mondays, so on the way in and out we fist bump and shout aiii whats good g fuck childrens services, and it feels a bit like were in pen getting kept away from each other cos were like mad dangerous gang leaders or some shit and if they leave us together were gonna take over the whole place and no one can stop us, but actually you just gotta get creative, like sometimes i borrowed some piss and took it along in a can of monster, and someone said drink a litre of vinegar, but i tried and just chucked it up

empty bottle service / ugh, its sticky
i remember back when i was in the old country in 39 degrees full sun and we drove a car that shook no belts no aircon, and at the side of the road there was always all these kids in fucked up clothes with the palest faces even though they lived in the sun and they walked in the filthy mud with the shittiest flipflops picking up bottles man thrown out the car, but still i swear, not all of them but some was still happy, smiling and laughing, and sometimes playfighting and throwing bottles and dunking in invisible hoops like it was soviet nba! and then i thought back to when we wasnt copping no ps and we needed snus or gina, and we walked round town picking up bottles for the deposit refunds too, and not gonna lie we was also pretty happy cos we was all working together for something and not doing that dark shit
and in a way it was a pretty good feeling

a question of guilt 2
the boys say to me, whats going on ivor youre so quiet you lost your voice or you swallow the joint and its not coming out again, and arjan says to me, ivor youre a different person, you never say nothing, when you gonna forget that gyal and get on with your life, and i was like, you reckon shes got on with her life, and marco went, no no no bro dont watch that, but i said, yeah, theres hundreds of gs out there shes probably banging one right now, and marco said quickly, no brother, shes sitting at home crying over you too, and it helped, i felt so much better, like, shukran marco my brother, then arjan said, or two, we was like, what you mean two, he said, two guys, she might be banging two

o hugs
so much is different here now just drugs drugs drugs
but never no hugs, mans got nuff floos, can get all the
dope man wants, but these days its not about wanting,
its about needing

one case worker was like, but you knew these were hard
substances when you started, i said, we never knew
what they was before we couldnt stop

real g
everything changes, the way you walk, stand, your facial expression, you smile less, laugh less, keep your eye on everyone, answer hard, you gotta be raw, closed, you start becoming someone else, lose yourself, and who knows if youre gonna find your way back

hourglass no sandy beach
im losing myself, every day that passes im disappearing like sand through fingers

starts with p and ends with d
and some things you dont tell no one even if maybe you should so instead they grow into massive ticking time bombs and ayla once said those things you call memories thats trauma

nono it was me who ended it
arjan was like, i met your ex in majorstuen yesterday, she got a new man, did you know? and she was asking hows ivor doing, i said good, hes got loads of women, and i laughed, like who remembers that gyal prehistoric times for real bro, then marco said, ivor, we gotta bounce, fix that thing remember, i was like right right, and we said later to the boys, got on the metro, and im crying and marcos like, you spoken to her since you broke up, i go no, marco says, call her, get it out of your system, say bye for real, im like why you saying this now, and he was just like, bruv, you got skeletons man still

i wrote a letter and marco put it in the post box, and i wrote honestly from the biggest muscle in my body aka my heart, sorry for the madness i got you caught up in you deserve better etc etc, then i said to marco, right look at me, im a better man step 9 here i come, marco said yeah bro, but i guess she wont

yeah bro, who the fuck needs females anyway
yesterday we was at some flash tings shubz and things
got a little fucked, so today i woke up to a situation and
a pounding headache and walked into the living room
where marco was lying with two gyaldem, i asked, bro,
where do you buy morning after pills is it the pharmacy,
marco laughed, what pharmacy, and pulled three packs
out of his bag

**dont stop it was just my boyfriend (wallahi who said i
was gonna)**
then marco and one girl was banging on the sofa, and
her phone starts ringing, must have rung twenty times,
in the end she answers like, fuck you want georg, for
fucks sake im busy!

ramadan
ramadan started this week so when we was in beirut i ordered three bab instead of four and marco went, bro aint you eating or what? so i said, no *youre* not eating or have you given up that lifestyle, he was like, bro, i already dont eat pork all year, that aint enough?

daydreams 1
i wonder how it feels when you die, is it like falling asleep late at night after a long day and the bed is soft and your eyes are heavy so you just float off on a soft pillow or is it like waking up at night after a nightmare and trying to fall back asleep but every time you close your eyes you open them again cos youre scared of whats waiting, i talked to the boys about it, jonas was like, honest to god, dying in your sleep must be the best, fuck dying in a car, if i gotta die, let me die in bed

17th may back in the day
i remember when we was little and marco had just come to norway and it was constitution day and warm and a pinup lolly cost ten kroner, and i said to him, bro, just wait till we get to town and you see all the seventeenth of may parades, its the guys who protect the king man, i swear you should be excited! and marco was excited, and so we reached town and it was full of people with balloons and big smiles and we had red silly string and sweaty suits that itched and didnt fit and norwegian flags and pinups that melted and sticky hands, and after wed been going round for an hour marco dashed his ice cream on the ground and shouted: the fuck, its just a load of potato face whiteys here, where are the shields and swords?

17th may back yesterday
after suits and lunch and booze and laughing at parades and sweaty feds we split for frogner park and sat with some peng tings, i went into the forest with one while jonas was telling the rest of the girls my stories, but i reckon hed drunk too much or some shit cos he was getting me mixed up with him . . .
marco and arjan took off, they came back with 7 pairs of sunglasses 5 airpods and 8 phones like, yalla habibi time to bounce

im telling you, those people gonna fuck with your head wallahi
been chatting with youth psych lately, childrens services said youre damaged so you need to get there or well fuck you over, i chatted with this lady, swedish, but shes aight so its no stress

she says i got some stuff, did one of them calculations or whatever, filled out a form and shit, crossing things off, answering questions, what do you eat, when do you sleep, are you a stressed person, does doing fun stuff make you happy, shit like that

then she was like, youre depressed, you have anxiety, you can keep on coming here, we might start you on some medication, but if so well need to be sure youre not getting high, i said aight, i wont get high, she was like ok, well hold off on the medication for a while

fear the king, long live the queen (he saw it in a film)
one of the olders who taught us things and that, hes
a little unstable a little crazy get me, so in the end
something had to go wrong and it did that weekend
when marco was at a shubz at my mans place, chugging
juice so he could just about stand, so then he goes to
the bathroom, falls into the washing machine so it tips
over, and under it is a bag, and in this bag theres two
point one million kroner headed for a dutch import
deal, and marco, whos fucked and fucking tired, just
takes the paper and bounces, which is not a smart thing
to do cos he dont put the washing machine back or
nothing, not exactly sherlock holmes level to figure out
whodunnit, and when my man sees the ps is gone, he
grabs a sten gun six lines of coke and a beretta and gets
in the car to go look for marco, luckily his gyal managed
to calm him down enough so marco was allowed to give
the ps back in return for a minor beating and a little
community service, but i told marco, if it hadnt been for
that woman, youd be dead now, he just shrugged, what
can i say, craignez le roi, vive la reine

first time for everything 2
jonas lost his virginity yesterday, we asked how it was,
he was like, dry tight and short we tried doggy but her
head hit the wall it went bop bop bop

jungle telegraph
we was sitting in beirut eating kingkong with fries and soda when marco shouted AWWWWWW so loud the birds flew into the air and ali behind the counter dropped the bab in the sauce shouted khalas and gave him a look like daggers, but marco almost didnt notice, just a quick sorry ammo, and then back to a state of shock staring at his phone,
i asked whats up, and he was like, you know that guy from that place, yeah he just got shanked, they badded man up, check this video, he got wetted, bumped wallahi, done for

young man short life
the video marco got on snap was already spread like a sheet on a double bed everywhere in stories and group chats, so the last seconds and minutes of mans life went viral, and even though vg nrk and tv2 said the feds was still trying to survey the situation, half of oslo already knew who what why, and even if the lawyer would say the familys in shock and cant understand why someone would do this to their son, no ones as innocent as wed like to think

two flies with one stone
usually wed be deep in discussion about whats gonna happen now, is anyone gonna try and retaliate, are them man gonna get grabbed, did he deserve it etc, but today no one had a single word on their tongues right up until jonas, whos always gotta be a joker at the worst moments, opens his mouth and says in this tiny squeaky voice: so he got his street confirmation and funeral in one, not bad

nightmare
woke up in darkness, eyes twitching, ears pounding, windows closed, room silent, bed creaking, birds tweeting, everythings getting stronger, theyre shrieking, shouting, theres a crash, head hits the ground, gravel scrapes my face, get up, back cracks, hit grass, earth in my mouth, blood in my mouth, they laugh, i feel the cold metal on the inside of my cheek, smell the cigarette, its marlboro red

shards of glass
some things you dont tell no one, like how even though the boys wanna be you and the gyals wanna be with you, sometimes you hang the biggest towel you can find over the mirror on the wardrobe in your room cos more than anything you wanna smash in the face of the brother staring back at you

counsel for the prosecution: high risk of repeat offending
woman in black like blah blah blah something that is heightened by the accuseds lack of impulse control and deeply reactionary nature, marco stood up and said, if someone spat in your face, wouldnt you punch them? who the fuck dropped you on your head

new times
we was at some mad shubz all the guys, and i dunno what happened, but maybe there was too much vodka and molly in my body cos the night turned into this big black hole until suddenly i was standing in the living room with half my hand up this shorty, and all the boys are like the fuck ivor, and marcos staring and the rooms silent, and even if this ting was smiling, i wasnt, cos now i realised this shorty was one marco been trying to chirpse for like two years, and tonight was going to be the night, so i left her alone and started saying, bruv i dunno whats what, but marco just shook his head and pointed at the door, he said, just get out of here ivor, youre embarrassing yourself wallahi

the next day i called marco, he was like, what is it? i said, sorry bruv, swear down i didnt clock it was her, its not about the girl ivor, its you, i cant trust you no more

no ocb
we got closest to death not with overdoses shanks or beef about money, but when marco wanted to blaze but was out of thins so instead he took two pages from the koran in the school library and put up a video on his story of him billing a zoot with them, and after school we met up in majorstuen to get some munch, i was like lets reach beirut, but marco was like, no brother no, i said whats going on, he was like, wallah bro i fucked up, cos apparently some man had screen recorded and the story was everywhere, and he showed me his snap, at least sixty man added him in two hours, and the chats was maaaadness still, you shoulda seen it, just like one death threat after the other, it was almost charlie hebdo for us you get me

moving out party
this brother in my class spent the whole time chatting about how he wished he had floos, would do anything for floos etc, and i got so sick of all his chat you cant imagine, fucking radio with no off button that man, in the end i had enough, i said, you want money, here, meet me after school youll get twenty-five, if you sort it, next time youll get fifty, i sent the address on wickr, and after school my man rocks up, trying to play it cool, but any man could see he was shaking like it was snow and minus twenty, i told him, listen everyones blazing, its easy work, i showed him this is a g, this is three point five, if you give out point eight per gram, your floos is gonna be a little better, he took the bar and asked if he could go, i said yeah, youll get a little longer cos this is your first time, but remember in two weeks ill be needing my paper, and if not, its gonna be a madness, and if you play me, ill find you

to begin with it went well, 25 turned into 50 turned into 100, but then he got jacked, and instead of finding a solution, he hid, stopped coming to school like a little dickhead, so i had to find him, after that he switched school, but i didnt know where, so i reached his flat two time, first i went off on his brother, then his old man

the second time, then i found out which school, we
stood outside for four days without this man showing
up, we reached his flat again with a habat, me, marco
and this other guy, he lived in a terraced house, we got
there, banged on the door, no answer, in the end this
neighbour comes past, said they was on holiday, i was
like, holiday yeah, what holiday? we tagged a target on
his window, you know, a red circle with a little plus sign
in the middle

it wound up with them reporting it, and the case took
almost five weeks, but in the end they dismissed it, and
he and his fam moved to the countryside

oslo paralympics
and sometimes i think about how things would have been if we was more normal, thats like the only thing me and marco cant chat about, one time i said to him have you thought about how we could have handled things differently? and he got so mad like, oh handled things differently you coulda been a philosopher or what, become a physiotherapist in that school of yours or what, stopped being able to handle it after you got wetted or what, the fuck you mean handled differently ivor, you been handling things this whole time, have you not, the kebab eat your fingers or something

private broker
the big brother of this guy who owes marco money
called me like, ivor marcos going off, can we talk it over please
i said to him, talk about what my friend, am i your therapist? your bro owes floos, until he delivers
he aint safe

worked to the bone
someone owes me money, someone jacked my little bro, someone snitched, someone pulled some shit, can you help me or what? sort it quick yeah? like i get youre busy, maybe someone you know, you gotta know someone, im just asking, i didnt mean that, allow it, how much, oh ah yeah i get it, nah thats fine, youll get a call at the weekend

curtains
this norwegian whitey friend of arjans was in a beef with some next man and wanted to scare them a little, so he reached to borrow silah, we was in somebodys yard, marco in the bedroom getting ready, and me and my man in the living room waiting all calm and serene, i was on a comedown, and marco was slow, and as a bonus the worlds biggest insect was flying around above us

it was like bzzzzzzzz

i said to him you know the name of that, he shook his head, i said mosquitos grandaddy, he was like, fuck you talking about mosquitoes for, can you sort it or not

marco come in with the gat, he said, close the fucking curtains, for fucks sake someones gonna see

third degree
i was in grønland and ran into a friend from little school
and cos this guy used to be a proper neeky nerd, i asked
what you doing here, and he said he was there cos he
needed a special banana for a first course and they only
have it in grønland

after that i said to him, lets link some day and catch up,
but he was like, uhuhuh, i said, wagwan, your tongue
get stuck today, he was like, i dont think its such a good
idea ivor, i dont wanna get . . . mixed up in anything,
i said to him, fam, whats going on with you, playing
distant with me and that, what you mean mixed up?
are you ribena or what, 4-to-1 with water, he was like,
no ivor, but i hear things, we all hear things you know,
people talk and that, i said talk about what, but he was
like, what happened to you bro, you remember when
we was little? i shouted, fuck that shit, he jumped and
i took off, he shouted to my back, be careful ivor, play
with fire youll get burned but play in the fire you might
be the one burning

you cant be trusted no more
swear down, today marco freaked at me like never before, thing is, jonas been having beef with some next man in his hood so he dont like walking home alone cos then they fuck with him, so me and marco been taking it in turns to walk him home, cos when were there, people suddenly turn invisible and vanish from the streets, and today it was my turn, but when i got home i took a few caps of gina and a xannie bar cos i was done in, and suddenly i woke up and it was nine oclock with twelve unanswered calls from marco and jonas, i called marco first, before i said a word he yelled: ivor, you fucking idiot, they jumped jonas! where the fuck were you?

grandma 1
jonas pops was away so the crib was empty, but since
lately we kept using it for shubzing, now he had to stay
with his grandma, but his grandma is kind and she
trusts him, so she said, ok, you go out with your friends
then, so he did, and we went over to the flat like fools
and got on a madness so the neighbours complained
and all hell broke loose, and marco almost got into a
fight with this neighbour lady, and suddenly the feds
turned up and called grandma, and it seems like that
was too much cos she had a heart attack
and died

grandma 2
we was in town when jonas got the call, with the guys from the shubz, not many, maybe ten, but you know, just us partying is enough to cause harakat

but now we was silent still, wed never been so quiet before, there wasnt a word to say in the whole world, arjan was crying, i aint never cried so much, just, jonas, jonas, sorry, and at the side of the street marco stood sharing out floos and breezers, jonas looked like his soul been taken, i swear, and i know we fuck around like oh hes so pale, but no i mean, now he was seethrough

me and marco kept quiet, meant to be the grownups innit, but it was like the world wasnt real, like we was floating on a bubble, maybe if we didnt speak it wouldnt break you know, and maybe it wouldnt have either, but this one guy from the shubz thought it was a prank, so he starts grinning like haha funny joke boys, like, his grandmas dead, yeah yeah sure, but marco aint feeling that so much, he starts shouting, in the middle of the platform at majorstuen, like hes grinning, hes grinning, the fuck you grinning for, you think its funny, and then the dude just grinned even more cos he didnt clock it was serious, so marco sparked him out

grandma 3
man was fine, i chatted to him, like listen, go home and shut up, he went c-c-course man, you you you know im not messing with you

grandma 4
that was a few weeks back, and after he lost his grandma, jonas was different, and not just different in a normal way like everyone gets when someone passes, but proper dark like someone turned off the light, and swear to god mans making me nervous cos he hardly ever comes out now, just sits at home blazing, he used to cough when he smoked, didnt inhale, and now hes blazing alone, whats going on?
and hes messing with other stuff, necking pills and shit, i say to people, dont shot to him, they say fine, even if i know its like putting an ice cube on a massive fire, and yesterday i called him, zero, so i left a message, i said stay off the pills bro, you dont know whats in them, one day you wont wake up

happy families 3
jonas pops is chaos, im telling you

sometimes we was there when his pops went off, he said to us get out, get out, yeah, but jonas had to stay, then his pops locked the door, and we sat in the stairwell listening to him getting bashed up in the living room

bam bam bam!

walk in the woods
it was early morning, and jonas was sitting on the back seat cos wed picked him up in the car from his mums and were on the way back to the city to munch a little breakfast, when we saw one of them man whod jumped him walking out of the shop by the metro, and he saw us, the sun was out, he looked over at the car we was in and then sprinted, i drove after, marco shouted YALLA HABIBI as i drove right into a row of wheelie bins ten or twelve metres in front of the guy, marco leaped out with the gat in his hand, he screamed, come here you fucking cunt, come here before i shoot you

and my man was stressing out all the way up to the forest, we said to him, dig, dig with your hands, that was when he started crying, no, no, arjuk ya allah saidni, please please, in the end man just collapsed, just put his arms around his head and shook, marco started kicking earth at him, it mostly looked jokes cos the ground was hard, like two crumbs came up for every kick, in the end we was like aight, get up, well take you home, you shoulda seen his face then i swear, like he didnt know if he should cry, or reach baker hansen and eat a cookie, after ten minutes in the car he started shaking and breathing like there was no air, so someone had to stuff some ksalol up his nose

1000 yard stare
we drove to bygdøy after that, the sun was setting, we had a joint, vodka, jonas sat on a stone and shivered, drank, eyes closed, tears on his cheek

when the cup is full . . .
it was evening, we was tired and i was ringing exes and girls who should have been exes, while marco rang people we had beef with and when the list was empty, people he thought we shoulda had beef with, arjan rang peppes, jonas rang his mother, he said, i want to come home, mum i want to come home

when the lights go off
when its evening and night and the shubz is over and facetime is over and everyones gone to bed except me cos i cant sleep and the high is wearing off, then i remember im totally alone

one day at a time until the very end
you tell me you dont want to live no more and i tell you
its gonna get better, it always gets better, and one day
you gonna look back happy you didnt leave, and you
ask, do you believe that yourself, and i dont wanna lie,
so i say, nah, but its true still

. . . you empty it
jonas called me with a happy voice like right at the start
when we met and he could still light up the spectrum
if you gave him time, and even though we hadnt spoke
for a few days, all i managed to say was yo, cos the boy
opened his mouth and started laughing, he said, broooo
im gonna m-move im gonna move im gonna move,
the old lady sorted a flat with a bathtub balcony and a
room for me, im not gonna live with my pops no more,
im going home to mum, home to my brother, and then
he stopped, and i had to laugh too, i said, congrats bro
mashallah, where you moving to, he said, oslo man, so
i can still hang out with the boys! and my heart sank,
dunno why

valkyrie plass
we sat on a bench in valkyrie plass trading teefed beer with rollies and stories from the alkies, marco was grinding chronic, and arjan made a roach, while jonas was grimacing from a big hit of gina, one of the alkies was called steinar and had a red nose and few words, but now he opened his mouth and asked jonas why he kept pouring that shit down his throat, and then jonas thought for a bit, but in the end he said for the pain, and steinar said, youre alive man, aint no medicine for that

THE EXCEPTION

starvation
we blazed some lemon haze and then bounced to the ghetto maccie ds in central station for burger and fries, but since arjan was broke he didnt get nothing for himself even though marco asked several times, you want some, you want some, its fine, ill tell them yours gotta be without mustard since you dont like it, but no, arjan was still proud, shaking his head, so in the end marco went, fine you dont want none, wafart, and we reached gøtke and ate, but when we was halfway through our burgers, arjan was like, yo let me have a taste, and obviously marco freaked and shouted, what did i say, what did i say, of course the starving indians gotta taste it, and after that he dissed arjan raw and slapped him on the forehead, but then out of the bag he pulled a hot burger no mustard

◯

marco ran into a yute whos eleven and who knows about us cos apparently we went to the same little school and he was in year four or something when we was in year eight, but when he saw marco now, first thing he said was, i need a job, i need a job, but marco said to him, what bro you got a vitamin deficiency, and this kid was like, huh, marco said, you cant even go on all the rides at tusenfryd and youre talking about a job, theres gotta be something missing from your diet, and this kid replies, my mums sick cant work so now my little brother aint got enough to buy lunch, and marco said he didnt exactly know what to say except: this aint the way to go, you blink three times and your little bros eating lunch on the way to visiting hours

when you wake up and realise it wasnt a dream
you know when you try to prepare for something, so in your head you picture it so many times its almost like it happened even though it didnt, and when it actually happens, its a bit like meeting a celeb youve seen a thousand times in interviews and on tv and you think in a way you know him a little still, but you actually dont, and you realise however many times you imagine something it will never be the same and you can never be ready

gone
people always say they felt it, like they woke up with
a bad feeling in their gut, and when they look back
everything makes sense and blah blah blah, but if youd
asked me the day before how he was doing, i woulda
said, good man

brother
last night i got woke up by marco ringing, and he was crying, he said, he died ivor, he died, and i didnt need to hear who to know, i just hung up, but he called back he said, jonas man, his dad found him ivor, jonas is dead

my darling
her whole body was shaking as they lowered the coffin,
in the church we talked to his little brother, he said
mum aint mum anymore,
she died with him

we saw it at the funeral when she fell
and someone was holding her up
it was his little brother
he was smaller than her

hopeless questions that dont have answers
most of all i wonder if he felt alone
he hated being alone

boom
whats worse, when they die slowly like a beautiful
flower withering, or sudden with no warning like
bombs exploding and turning the world into a confused
chaos of dust, shards of glass and ringing in your ears

ALL MY BOYS ARE ON GHB
we was on the metro with our first litre of ghb, big day, we was happy then get me, it was early days, things was still fun, every day started with the feeling of not knowing what might happen, every day a new adventure, we started singing and clapping, all of us on the train,
jonas was dancing

all my boys are on G-H-B
all my boys are on G-H-B

below zero
id been out drinking with the boys and was on the way home and it was two oclock my phone dead my high fading, so i went to check a couple of shottas and rang the doorbell, but they wasnt home and i was on the way to a third when i ran into some cats we know in the parking lot at gunerius, and i said, yo you got anything, they said, just this, and id never tried it before, but fuck it, so i paid up, and they baked up, and when it hit, i finally felt like i was home

daydreams 2
marco said, if you had infinite amounts of one kind of dope how would it end, i said, speed would be psychosis ghb straight to the grave ecstasy liver failure heroin living my best life and alcohol quick double murder and go flying in front of the train

ten signs of a healthy psyche
i woke up in an unfamiliar bed with an unfamiliar chick,
i asked where i was, she said holbergs plass, i asked if wed done anything, she said no, just coke and booze, first you were stressed out, then you were smashed, and then you didnt want to fuck, just cried about some friend of yours, she said, you got any more coke by the way, i shook my head, she was like, ok, then i think you should go

red bull gives you wings
i was on the way home and my head was chaos, and the screen said now, and the train thundered in the tunnel, so i made up my mind, got ready, jumped and got pulled back by my hood while the train exploded in front of my eyes, a man shouted, what are you doing, i was like, fuck you yeah mind your own business

nature or nurture 2
this shotta arjan knows sent a snap, he said, your mates
little brother was here copping weed off me just fyi,
i remember one time jonas facetimed with his little
brother and his old lady, was trying to hide the fact he
was blazed, but i remember his mum said, jonas, are you
high my boy, are things that bad?
and jonas knew she knew, but with his little brother
it was something else, he said it every time we was
chugging or dropping mandy, first hed get high, then
hed get muslim, hed be like, my little brothers never
touching this shit here wallahi, never!

mum
we say the old lady, so we dont have to say mum, the old ladys going off, instead of mums worried, mums worried about me

lungs full of water
its not stages anymore, its waves
better and worse, better and worse
its not stages of grief anymore, said youth psych,
its waves
i thought, i guess you read that in a good book, but
forget waves,
im just drowning

the old lady
i was on my way out the door, the old lady asked,
where you off to, out, where, town, then silence, she
looked so tired, said please come home again, i nodded,
ill come home

red bull 2
marco freaked, i didnt actually mean to say nothing about the train, like what did it have to do with him, but then we dropped some acid together and soon i was thinking it was a funny story, anything can be funny, so i tried telling it with some jokes

at the end he opened his mouth and his voice was low, he was like, the fuck im gonna do with you ivor, you need help for real, i said, bro chill, im just kidding, but marco looked at me, he whispered, dont lie ivor, youre not kidding, and i almost whispered too, i said yeah it was a joke, what do you think, do i look like kurt cobain or something, am i that much of a fool, and then he said, say wallahi it was jokes, so i said wallahi knife to my throat and cross my heart ten times i was playing, and then marco finally smiled and said aight

marcos old lady
today marcos old lady got threatened by this guy we got beef with, basically marco wasnt home, but she was, so i reached marco to link up and find a solution, but when i came up the stairs, marco was standing in the stairwell and his mum was above him shaking and crying, she screamed: if you want to go and be a junkie on brugata or a murderer in prison, do it, do what you want liban, youre my only son, but youre crushing me, i dont want to see you here again

happy ending
boom boom boom, open up, police!!! three cars, five
feds, eight in the morning, habats and all

after they got me on the floor and i seen the paper, one
started rummaging and digging around in my room,
another took my phone, checked my clothes and said
no, you dont need to get dressed, so i sat on the floor
in my boxers freezing my tits off while the others was
standing over me their faces looking all bunged up
like they just drank too much milk or some shit, and
i said to them, aint the feds unarmed? they was like,
yeah normally, and in my head i was thinking, are they
dumb? they think ima pop a fed? and then i thought
about that one man in grønland who they popped, fuck
that still, but at the same time i felt kinda hard, cos
marco got raided a few times lately too, but then it was
more like two plainclothes guys, and after they drank
coffee and asked how life was

one of the guys sat down beside me and started the
whole good cop show like, im here to help you, but i
was already laughing, i said, bro, if youre here to help
me why aint i lying on a massage table with a little asian
ting getting a happy ending

the boys
they raided marco and arjan later that day, but of course they knew and had tidied up, so when the feds came, they filmed and uploaded to stories with the caption like hahaha FTP 1312 😂😂 marco even facetimed us while they was there, so it was all good

marco
they took marco in and talked to him, fucking waste of taxpayers money, that man aint talked to feds since he learned norwegian, one time the feds came to his place, his old lady said, please, talk to them, but marco went, no ill eat my tongue before i talk to khanzir, but if jonas was here, wed have been fucked, good and proper, that guy was too easily led, he would hear *were just trying to help him* one time, and he would have texted like, ivor, i told them everything, youre welcome 😊 👍

houseshare
the feds called in on one of the gyals, she lives in a houseshare and they tore her room apart and her friends was like, whats going on, but they didnt find nothing, and after she called me and left a voicemail, freaking all tears and that, like, the police at my place ah ah ah ah fuck you you promised

when life becomes numbers and numbers become life
after that i answered, and she said ivor they kicked
in my door, this is not ok, i said, ok let me know how
much it was ill vipps it over, she was like, im not a
whore, im not ringing you to get paid, you promised,
the fuck is wrong with you?

everything you never got to see
and sometimes a funny thought occurs to me and in
my head i smile and think oof i gotta remember to tell
jonas about that but then i remember jonas aint here
no more

and i remember one time you said you looked forward
to being an adult with children who was adults too
cos then you would know for sure they was done with
childhood and alhamdulillah, it was better than yours

ekeberg park
and i bet marco and arjan think about him a lot too,
but i dont know cos we never say nothing, only when
were so fucked we know we wont remember too much
the next day, then maybe we say a little, like two days
ago we was dragon chasing and in the end we was lying
in ekeberg park too charged to walk or crawl, but then
like a bolt from the blue arjan calls out, jonas, first
quietly, then louder and louder like a phone alarm again
and again without stopping, and in the end he was
shrieking, and marco started too, and it sounded like
people in the videos from the war in ukraine when they
find a little red shoe outside a collapsed building and
they recognise it

man dont imagine its sick to pop benzos its fucking raw
arjan was visiting his mum yesterday and she found a roach behind the house and went to his room to freak out but when she came in he was wrapped in his duvet under the bed with graveyard shifts on repeat which no arguments is an all time top five norwegian song, the only problem was that he wasnt breathing so his old lady started crying and shrieking so his stepfather came and dialled 113 and apparently arjan had smuggled in a bottle of xannies and decided to take them all but anyway it went ok hes in the hospital now it was bad luck

fališ mi jako
i still remember ayla being like, you talk about your grandma a lot, do you really miss her? she said, i wish i could have met her, its a shame shes not here, i went, im glad she didnt have to see how everything turned out, ayla was like, but maybe it wouldnt have gone like this if she was here, and its not too late

nights down low
she baked buns for me bro, homemade with a piece of chocolate in the middle and left to rise in her shared kitchen,
no girl ever did nothing like that for me you know,
she even said, if you want to go on earning money like you do regardless, at least save some up for something, study after school, buy a flat, and when we was discussing something, she never let me off the hook either, even though most give in quickly or never start

the lawyer 1
and i talked to the lawyer, he said theyre trying to get me for a lot of things, he was like, no, its not looking all that rosy, i must admit, and if youre found guilty of all that, then . . . i said then what, he was like, no, lets not focus on that, and he didnt know much more, but i got it, buckle up, winter is coming

the lawyer 2
and i was like, its funny im here now, cos when i was younger i wanted to be a lawyer, and the guy said, but not if you carry on like this

block
i was outside jonas block today, his neighbours said hi,
even the ones who used to hate us, the feds stopped me
too, they was friendlier than usual, they said: its sad,
good kid la la la, hows things with you, its not good
that life

the lawyer 3
a few days later the lawyer called and said come by cos
he got some new info, insights, charges and that, so i
sat in the white office brown chair as he read through
his thin glasses like, import, sale, paragraph 337, 341,
the guy read on, didnt say much, aggravated robbery,
kidnapping, he was done in the end, he said, if you go
down for this, ivor, were talking years

and im waiting to see you call
i still have your contact in my list, in favourites on the first page there, so your pale face pops up every time i go to call someone, it was the picture i took a long time ago on the steps you know, that time

i think a lot about that evening, what would have happened if marco hadnt brought me along?

maybe you would be finishing the second year of college now, just one year left, like woohoo apprenticeship here i come! you woulda been celebrating now for sure, having a few beers or something, throwing up your mcchicken on the pavement with your other normal friends, im sure youd have found some in the end

at the weekends you probably woulda played board games or some shit, those little miniatures, and i swear you already woulda planned what to do with your first floos from your apprenticeship stuff, like awww six big ones! wow so much money!!!

and when i visited marco at school you probably woulda walked past us and looked at the ground, like hope they

dont fuck with me, and i reckon we woulda fucked with
you too, like just a little
but still it woulda been better that way,
no?

driven out
ill be out in a minute, said arjan
its dark, i can see people behind us, i say to marco can
you drive out? drive the fucking car! breath ragged,
hands sweating, i pull at the door, open up, open up!
marco rolls down the window, sticks his head out
hey! he shouts
the guys answer
you live next door to the childrens home, right?
the guys nod
marco turns to me
you see ivor? nothing to be afraid of, and look,
theres arjan

maybe not everyone needs to learn the hard way
we reached a shubz later that night, and i chatted to
a few different people and downed a few shots and i
ended up where i most like to be which is on the terrace
alone with quiet music through the glass door and a
view of lights and red buses, and i was in the middle of
a nicotine rush and billing a jay, when the door opened
and this girl came out, she looked a year younger than
us, sat down and asked, can i have some? i nodded,
passed the joint and asked you blazed before, and she
went, yeah yeah of course, but then she coughed up
half a lung at ninety decibels and was like, no, actually i
havent

and we sat a while talking, but i dont think shed
chugged that much before cos suddenly her head
switched off and she started laughing and talking in
this irritating way, so i said, lets have a gerro and be
quiet, and for maybe fifteen minutes we just sat on
the veranda smoking tabs, but in the end she looked at
me with her head swaying and asked in this low gyal-
is-ready voice, you do dangerous things, dont you?
and even though i didnt reply, she took it as a yes and
started asking more, and i know how it goes or at least
how it could go, and in my mind i was thinking sure,

why not, but then marco came out, and i dont know
who hacked his brain but this man pulled me inside,
and as he was closing the door, he turned to this girl
and said, there are good guys and bad ones, dont waste
yourself on one whos just collecting stories

rope or bathtub
marcos nephew got corned, so today marco was at the funeral and half nine at night he came into beirut in this black hugo boss suit like some mad raw denzel/john wick with a mad empty polish vodka bottle, and under his shirt the vest was bulging, and he laughed, smiled and was fucked and fucking happy, and in the end he put his head back like he was asleep, and arjan went out for a gerro and asked, you coming? but i said no, and when he was outside, marco lifted his head and whispered, if this life dont kill me soon, i swear ima do it myself

bad luck
and after that he told a joke, we laughed, i was feeling sick, but then we had our first proper chat about jonas, like its easier if you laugh first

anyway we talked for a few minutes about jonas, missing him, funny things we remembered, in the end i said, the world is an unfair place, imagine a little bad luck creating so much chaos and marco shook his head like, what bad luck ivor? drop it wallahi, you know as well as i do

xabsi
i was in the hallway after school when this one man i know was like ivor, you getting lockup or what, and i said, what you mean lockup? he said, i was with the feds the other day, questioning about a robbery, and they was asking about you, whos he sell to, who works for him, i said i didnt know you, they said good, cos hes not gonna be out much longer

burnt rubber and singed leather
and some things you dont tell no one, like how the ps
and gyals and puffas and watches could have happily
burned like a bonfire on saint johns if only man could
take back mums tears

mxe
after beirut we was tripping on some shit weve not tried before called mxe thats meant to be like ketamine but it went as fucked as it could cos arjan vanished and we still aint found him

free men
things didnt go brilliantly, cos after three hours arjan got grabbed, and marco said hed got lost in a residential area with big houses, and i dont even know where that could be, cos where we was, there was no big houses, arjan had laid down in a garden, and suddenly all the people in their big houses was calling askar who came and freaked and rang the home, who came right along, and even if they had no one to ring, they freaked an all, and then arjan was on a serious bad trip, and according to marco, he was freaking out pretty bad too, cos he shouted at the people from the home that hed taken mxe and lsd and he was gonna keep on doing that, and no one can stop him cos hes a free man, and to be honest that wasnt so smart, cos even if all of us should be free men, arjan only is when the home says he is, and they dont say it that often and especially not when hes wasted and screaming, and arjan knows that, so on the way to the home they stopped to get

petrol, and the support workers said to arjan, stay in the car, and he said fine, and he stayed in the car like they said, but also he climbed into the drivers seat and drove, and he sent a video to the group chat looking like hindi prison break with this huge smile and the speakers were playing happy-clap-along-if-you-feel and he got three minutes along the e6 before crashing and now the home has sent him out of oslo and he aint coming back

the ladder 2
my friend who climbed the ladder and saved my life
in year ten called today and said lets get together, and
we did, and he told me hed quit college and started
working in sales for this big company and is making
sixty gs a month, and the team hes in, he says its the
wackest boys club, and the deputy manager is a playboy
with a load of zeros in his salary and tinder on lock,
and theres this ice hockey dude whos twenty years old
totally on one, and didnt hear about the rules before
he started, and not after either, and my friend said,
you two would have been a dangerous duo, and you
can already sell, just think how well you coulda done
if you didnt have to stress, and i can talk to my boss,
it could be a new start away from the streets, but still
loads of floos, and you dont need to make a decision
now, but think about it and call me yeah, just promise
me youll call? and my boss is called lars and hes the best
i ever had

mashallah
after we met i went into the turkish shop in grønland and was buying a mango lassi when suddenly i heard, ivor! and with my hand around the gat in my bag i turned around ready for anything, but actually i wasnt ready for this, cos in front of me was this old brudda i aint seen for like two years, and the last time we saw each other, he was asleep in middelalder park with a needle in his arm and an 11 month sentence just round the corner, so now he was standing in front of me, i almost didnt recognise him in these nice clothes, buff tan and huge grin, i said, ya akhi whats good, you get the worlds biggest glowup or what? and his mum was there too cos they was shopping together (he definitely didnt have no beefs running), and she said, yeah isnt he handsome, working and taking care of his family mashallah god is good, and the guy grinned and said thanks, then he pulled me to one side, he said, ivor, people been talking, the way youre living man, not working wallahi, time to pattern up

faith>earth
its been six weeks since arjan was moved
and four months since jonas

we havent spoken to arjan so much since he took off,
cos the thing is they put him in a proper dope home,
a fucking junkie houseshare yeah, kid he lives with is
a proper pillhead, someones on needles, so it was just
more dope innit, he bummed a bunch to begin with, we
vippsed him, sent up a little floos, but now its getting to
a round forty like, bro its not happening, so we stopped,
after that he freaked, la la la, things got dicey man, i
ran into this one man who knows people up there, he
was like, you heard about your brudda, turned into a
junkie innit

things changed around here too, marco started reaching
mosque a bit, praying more and that, writing rap like,
sick of my life going south so now i pray to the east,
but hes been a druggie since he was in nappies, so
stoppings a process get me, and lately his mum got sick
and that, burned out they say, anxiety, insomnia and
shit, so marcos well angry, guilty conscience maybe, for
instance the other day he got arrested in the park after
badding up two security with a skateboard, but hes

trying at least, he said, im done wallahi, ima be a better man for god and for my family, you know, its not here and now, he said
its deen over dunya

BACK IN THE DAY
we was lying in the net on the pier, in the little bit of
the oslo fjord called pipervika
the lawyer had called two hours earlier, he said:
i dont know what happened, but the case has been
closed.
you were lucky this time, ivor

marco asked, what you gonna do now the case is done?
i just shrugged, well see bro, maybe get a job still, some
legal ting, marco laughed, what you mean legal bruv?
legal ting, you?? some sales ting, i said, chatting on the
phone and that

after a few minutes he cleared his throat and said: we
was sure it was the end, you know? wallahi me and
arjan were sure, now theyre gonna pass some long
sentence, now ivors getting banged up, boom khalas,
see you in twenty-four

i closed my eyes,
it was better back in the day, dont you think?
marco looked at me, he grinned
in a way, but i think its gonna be better when were
older, still

the exception
after that i had a meeting with the dude from childrens services,
bro, tired offices there no lie, i dont fuck with that

as per the guy there was giving lip, an hour forty-five minutes he nagged, fucking twice round the metro, mortensrud to tøyen times six he nagged, blah blah blah, but i think the guy finally realised that shit dont work on me, cos in the end he was just like, stop it, honest talk man, there aint no future as a junkie or a dealer, there aint no future, he said, as a rule it goes badly, as a rule they die

after that i met up with marco
i said im gonna be the exception to the rule

and

to Baba
i wish you could see me now